# BECAUSE
## THE
# NIGHT

# BECAUSE THE NIGHT

KYLIE SCOTT

Because the Night, Copyright © 2025 by Kylie Scott

All Rights Reserved. All rights reserved, including the right to reproduce this book or portions thereof in any form whatsoever. For information contact the copyright owner.

This is a work of fiction. Names, characters, places and incidents either are the product of the author's imagination or are used fictitiously. Any resemblance to actual persons, living or dead, events or locales is entirely coincidental.

Editor: Kelli Collins
Proof Reader: Elaine York, Allusion Publishing, www.allusionpublishing.com
Interior Book Design: Elaine York, Allusion Publishing, www.allusionpublishing.com
Cover Design: By Hang Le

ISBN: 978-0-6484573-9-8

"Lullaby" by The Cure
"Blossom" by It's Acrylic
"Hollywood's Bleeding" by Post Malone
"Bloodletting" by Concrete Blonde
"bury a friend" by Billie Eilish
"I Get A Kick Out Of You" by Ella Fitzgerald
"If We Were Vampires" by Jason Isbell and the 400 Unit
"Running Up That Hill" by Placebo
"Moonlight Sonata" by Beethoven
"Saturn" by SZA
"Dream A Little Dream" by Louis Armstrong
"The Hills" by The Weeknd
"Vampire" by Olivia Rodrigo
"I Am Not A Woman, I'm A God" by Halsey
"Cross Road Blues" by Robert Johnson
"Cry Little Sister" by Gerard McMahon
"Because The Night" by Patti Smith

## CHAPTER ONE

The house is protected by a tall, stone fence and hidden by an overgrown garden. Given the way the hinges of the wrought-iron gate screech when I push it open, I doubt anyone has been here in years. Which is weird. This Spanish Revival in the Hollywood Hills must be worth a fortune. A weed-infested gravel path leads to the large, arched, wooden front door. Three stories of white walls and terracotta roof tiles tower above me.

My boss, Jen, said to go through the place from top to bottom and make a note of anything that needed to be fixed. Any water leaks or signs of animals, etcetera. The Thorn Group doesn't normally provide this service. Guess the client is special.

Inside the house, the air is stale, and sheets cover much of the furniture. The place feels like a museum. It has all of the original features, wooden rafters on the high ceiling and French doors opening onto a courtyard. But the overall atmosphere is oppressive as fuck. When I sneeze from the dust, the sound echoes through the empty house. Same goes for my footsteps. The electricity works, but half of the bulbs are blown, and the other half are too dim to be useful. It all adds to the haunted house vibe.

I wander through room after room, carrying the set of heavy, old house keys, peering into corners and under shrouded chairs and tables. There's no security system, and yet the place hasn't been touched. It's nothing less than a miracle. A grand piano and a wall full of leather- and clothbound books take pride of place in the living room. Art and photos and antique mirrors hang on the walls. And a bar cart stocked with half-empty bottles of liquor sits beside the ornate fireplace full of ash. It looks like the owner just up and left—walked out mid-cocktail party or something.

The view is spectacular on the third-level balcony. All of the glamor and grime of the Sunset Strip. Streetlights flicker down below as the sun sinks in the west. There's an old saying about a red sunset. Some warning of the weather and things to come, but I can't remember what it is. A cold autumn breeze has me wrapping my cardigan tighter around me. Time to get this job done. There's a hot bath and a good book waiting for me at home. Though there's no food, so a grocery stop will be required. A salad from Trader Joe's sounds good, so does their sea salt brownie bites, because balance.

Taking notes on my cell, I move from room to room as night sets in. The house is in good condition for its age. And if I focus on my work, I can ignore its general spookiness—right up until a branch scrapes against a window, making me shriek.

*Shit.*

I rub the heel of my palm against my rib cage. My heart is hammering inside my chest. Jen not giving me urgent, last-minute jobs would be great. Exploring abandoned buildings with bad lighting is also officially not my thing. Something I might want to add to my contract moving forward. None of this situation should have happened. I entered Jen's office to ask for a raise, only to have her forget I scheduled the meeting and send me here.

Having walked through the upper, main, and lower levels (the latter of which is partially set into the hill), only the basement remains. Another of those weak lightbulbs barely illuminates the staircase. I have to force my feet to keep taking the next step and go down there.

The basement is about what I expected: a boiler and storage in one vast room. But the sheer amount of stuff down here is awe inspiring. Furniture and paintings and wooden chests. Endless racks of dusty old bottles of wine. It's like an antique store and a vineyard had a baby and that child chose chaos.

This is wild. Who owns all of this? How many generations did it take to collect it all?

I plod along, leaving footsteps in the dust. With the way the hairs on the back of my neck are standing at attention, it feels as if someone is watching me. Which is ridiculous. But then, I always did have an overactive imagination. If this were one of my true-crime podcasts, the psycho killer would absolutely be about to jump out and grab me. And each and every member of the audience would shake their heads and say what an idiot I was to enter the creepy basement. They would absolutely be right.

In the shadowy back corner is a locked door. It's made out of thick, scarred wood, as if the surface had been burnt and attacked over time. I don't want to know what's behind it. I don't even want to go near it. But I pull up my big girl panties and search the old ring of ornate keys for a match.

As much as I try to be quiet, the keys clink and scrape. Not that it matters—there's no one here but me. I remind myself of this fact over and over again. However, my shoulders rise higher and higher with each passing moment.

There are six keys. I try them all, testing them against the rock-solid lock. Until finally I am left with only one. Every fiber of my being is praying that it won't work. Meaning my job here is done and I can haul ass back home.

*Click.*

But no. The key turns and the sound of the lock releasing echoes around the room. I've heard screams that were quieter. My throat is so damn tight it's hard to breathe.

Nope. I can't do it. Jen can fire me for all I care. No way am I turning the handle and opening the door to see what's inside. I've never been a big believer in the unknown. But the bad vibes or whatever the hell they are rolling off of this door are too intense to be denied. I don't want to know what's back there. What I do know that I'm doing is getting out of here. Right now.

Having made the decision, my sense of relief is mighty.

A calm and reasonable person would take their time in the low lighting. Be careful not to trip over anything. But each step I take away from that door is faster than the last. The urge to vacate this place is now the only thing I am feeling.

As I near the staircase, a low, menacing growl comes from somewhere behind me. Next comes slow, shuffling footsteps.

This cannot be fucking happening. My thick thighs rub together beneath my skirt as I bolt for the staircase. Blood pounds a hectic beat behind my ears. Forget locking the house. I just flee. Up the stairs and out the door and through the garden and onto the street. And my car is right there—it's all going to be okay.

But two strong arms, like bands of steel, wrap around me from behind. There's a stinging pain in the side of my neck. Some deep, animal instinct tells me it's sharp, predatory teeth stabbing through my skin. I struggle and writhe; however, there's nothing I can do. My scream echoes down the empty street and into the uncaring night. No one is coming to save me.

The attack goes on and on, draining me of my strength, robbing me of my life. It doesn't hurt exactly, at least after the first sharp sting, but it sure as hell isn't pleasant feeling my life's blood drain away.

Dark spots float before my eyes as my heartbeat slows to next to nothing. I feel myself being lowered to the ground. The asphalt is cold and rough against my back, and yet my mind is peaceful. Is this what dying feels like?

A cool hand grabs hold of my chin and a disinterested blue gaze in a gaunt face looks me over. His lean features seem to be filling out before my eyes. A hint of color returns to his ashen skin. His teeth are white, even for California, but what's bizarre is the length and sharpness of his canines. Animals have teeth like that. And other things known for biting people and drinking blood do, too.

Things I don't want to name because they're impossible, and don't exist, and oh God.

"Everything is fine," he says, meeting my gaze.

And it's true. I should be terrified, but for some reason I'm not, and I don't understand why.

If I have to die, at least I'm doing so in the presence of beauty. Because he is breathtaking. Longish dark hair and white skin with a sharp jawline, angular cheekbones, and a high forehead. He looks like a Hollywood hero, and his suit is obviously vintage. I can tell by the wide lapels and baggy pants. It's as if he just stepped out of an old black-and-white movie. Something with James Dean or Jimmy Stewart, like my grandmother used to watch when I was a child.

For a long moment, he looks up. No idea if he's staring at the streetlight, the jet plane passing overhead, or even the blinking light from a satellite high in the night sky. But his gaze is thoughtful when he turns back to me. He looks over my face and figure with renewed interest.

"I don't know this world," he says, as if to himself. Then he strokes my cheek with the pad of his thumb, before winding a lock of my hair around his finger. "And you remind me of someone. What's your name?"

"Skye."

"Skye," he repeats in a pleasant tone. "You're going to be a good girl for me, aren't you, Skye?"

Of course, I am. I would do *anything* to please him. But when I try to nod, or to speak again, nothing happens. I simply lack the strength. My whole body feels light, insubstantial. Like I might float away on the next breeze. It's then that I realize I haven't even done anything interesting with my life, and here I am, about to lose it.

With a sigh, he brings his wrist to his mouth and bites. Then he presses the wound to my lips and says, "Drink."

Blood trickles into my mouth, the scent of copper and taste of iron is overwhelming. I barely manage to swallow, but I do because I wouldn't dare disobey him. A sharp sensation spreads through me, forcing its way into my flesh and bones. It is fire without heat, and it brutally consumes me.

When I try to turn my head, he forces me back, making me take more. I want to cry and scream and puke all at the same time. The blood flows down my throat and through my body and all I can do is lie there and...

"I know you're awake," says a deep, amused voice. "It's time we had a little talk."

I open my eyes a sliver. Just enough to see the linen bedsheet beneath my cheek and the shadows thrown by the thick candle burning on an antique wooden desk. I doubt this is Heaven. Not that I've ever been particularly religious. But when I imagined an afterlife, I pictured an eternal, peaceful darkness. A whole lot of nothing with all of my anxiety gone for good. A big old four-poster bed with a beautiful bastard sitting on a wingback chair in the corner watching me—not so much.

Though he could be the Devil. His presence is commanding as he sucks all of the air from the room. He radiates power and strength and I have never experienced anything like it. He has big dick energy to the nth.

"You attacked me. You fucking bit me." The strange thing is, I feel amazing. The best I have ever felt. Which makes no sense, and means I'm nowhere near as afraid of him as I should be. Confusion and righteous anger are my main emotions right now. "How long was I out?"

"Ladies don't swear."

"Ladies do what they like, and I happen to like salty language...a lot. Now answer the question."

"Not long." He holds up my cell. "What's this?"

"My phone."

His dark brows rise. "This is a telephone?"

"Yes. How do you not know that? Where am I?"

"In one of the basement rooms you were so clumsily trying to enter. It's little wonder you woke me," he says. "What year is it?"

I sit up and wrinkle my nose. "What year is it? Who are you, Sleeping Beauty?"

"Just answer the question." I tell him, and his response is, "Huh."

Something is definitely going on with me. My sight is somehow so much better. Even with only the low light of the solitary candle, I can see everything. From a couple of dust motes dancing in the air to the missed stitch on the collar of his button-down shirt. It's like looking through a magnifying glass. Seeing the world in such detail is overwhelming.

"Relax your eyes," he says. "Broaden your focus. It takes some getting used to."

"What did you do to me?"

"Have the old tales already been forgotten?"

Not only has my sight changed, but I can hear more things, too. An insect scuttling across the floor upstairs and a night bird calling in the garden. We're underground in a basement room with solid stone walls and no windows. There's no way I should know that a car is cruising past the other end of the street, or that a neighbor is playing "Saturn" by SZA.

My fingers tighten on the thick, woolen blanket thrown over the end of the bed, and the material tears as if it were wet paper. It's all too much. Scents, sights, sounds, touch, and taste. Everything has suddenly been amped up to eleven.

The asshole sighs. "You're going to break a lot of shit before you get yourself under control, aren't you?"

"What did you do to me?"

"You know." He smirks and rises to his feet. "I can see it in your eyes."

I don't know, but I do have my suspicions, as wild as they are. I run my tongue over my teeth and taste blood after one of my enhanced canines scratches it. "This is...vampires aren't real."

"If you say so," he says.

"It's not possible."

"Okay."

His amused gaze makes me want to scream. "I hate you."

"And now you have all the time in the world to do so. Isn't that nice?"

"Oh my God. You're serious."

"As the dead," he confirms.

"No. I won't kill people."

"You don't have to. Though, it takes practice to resist the urge to feed until you're satiated once the blood fills your senses." He snaps his fingers at me like I'm a dog. Asshole. "Enough of this. We have errands to run, and you'll be getting hungry soon. Come here, Skye."

There's an answering tug inside me at his words. An urge to do what he said. It's like an invisible, psychic thread linking us together.

"Look at me," he orders, gazing into my eyes. "Come here, Skye."

Once more, I feel the tug in the center of my chest. But, honestly, he can go to Hell. "I am not one of the undead, the whole idea is ridiculous. Because vampires wouldn't have panic attacks, and I'm clearly having one now. My life. My friends and family and job and—"

"Come here now." He doesn't raise his voice, but I have to cover my ears to protect them against the wall of sound that hits me. It echoes around inside my skull, all sharp edges. The agony of it is still echoing inside me as I climb off the bed. Not doing as he asks has consequences, apparently.

"That hurt," I whisper, massaging my temples. "Please don't do it again."

"So the sire bond does work on you, it just takes extra will on my part. That's going to be annoying."

"Sire bond?"

"I made you. Therefore, I'm your sire." He pushes his thick, dark hair back from his face and stares down at me. I am average height, but barely reach his broad shoulder. "Your old life is over. The best way to keep your friends and family safe is to stay away from them."

My go-fuck-yourself gaze says it all.

"You're more difficult to kill now, but it's not impossible." He circles me like a shark before taking hold of my ponytail and wrapping it tightly around his fist. Then he tugs, pulling me back against his hard body. "And make no mistake, I will end you if you don't start being useful and stop misbehaving. Do you understand?"

"Yes."

"Good." He releases me with a warning look. "Who sent you here tonight? How did you get the house keys?"

"My boss gave them to me."

"And who is your boss?"

"Are you going to hurt them if I tell you?"

He thinks it over for a second. "It's highly doubtful. I'd be more concerned about my own skin if I were you. Now... don't make me ask again."

"Jennifer Manning," I say reluctantly. "I work for a company called The Thorn Group."

He smiles. "The Thorn Group? Is that so?"

I glare at him.

Not that he cares. "Let's start there then. We have a lot of ground to cover before dawn."

## CHAPTER TWO

"Why me?" I ask as we drive through West Hollywood. "I needed a tour guide to this century and there you were."

"Great." I've spent my entire life never being chosen for anything. Being average height, average weight, and bookish, I tend to blend. Neither the cool kids, nor the jocks wanted anything to do with me in school, and men like him have looked straight past me ever since. "That's just great."

"People have begged me for the gift I just gave you. Offered me riches beyond imagination. Yet all you do is whine."

"Dude, you killed me. You actually killed me. Do you seriously expect me to thank you?"

"How long is it going to take for you to get past that?"

"I don't know," I say. "But when I do, we're going to have a long conversation about consent."

He shakes his head.

"When I was dying...you said something about me reminding you of someone?"

"I don't know what you're talking about."

Maybe I imagined it. My memories of the attack and him turning me are shadowy at best.

There are plenty of people out tonight, and so much traffic. He must have been awake sometime in the last century because he knows how to drive. And he drives my ten-year-old Prius so I don't accidentally break it. Like how I cracked the wood banister as we were heading out. All I did was put my hand on it and bang. I obviously don't know my own strength. Or speed, for that matter. Every move I make now needs to be slow and steady and careful. Given my general lack of patience, this is no easy feat.

The vehicle's keyless start and automatic transition were new to him. I also had to talk him through the various electronics. For a while, he just sat and stared at the dashboard in a daze. Guess there are a lot of lights and information. Now I stare out the passenger-side window in a similar state. I think I'm in shock. I know this is happening, but it doesn't seem real. Like I am watching it all from a distance.

"Women such as yourself used to be more accommodating," he says. "Less sharp-tongued."

"Women such as myself?" I ask archly.

He doesn't respond. But the word *homely* appears in a still and silent corner of my mind. And I absolutely bet it's what he means. Asshole.

"How long were you in that room for?"

"A while."

"Did we even have the right to vote the last time you were awake?"

"Yes. That happened in 1920," he says. "You don't wear a wedding ring. Are you a spinster or a widower?"

"Neither. I'm single. Spinster isn't a term that's used now."

"No boyfriend?"

"No. And no girlfriend or partner either."

"So you live with your family?"

I snort. "I have my own place. Thank you very much."

He does the furrowed forehead thing. Like he is judging all of my life decisions. Again.

"You may not realize it, but there have been multiple studies done proving that single women living alone are one of the happiest subsets of people in the world."

"Is that so? What does this button do?" He pushes something and music blares out of the stereo. A song by Halsey. "Is this if you want to torture someone at the same time as you're driving?"

"No, it's for enjoyment. Halsey's great."

We stop at a red light, and he examines the sports car beside us with interest—along with the handsome Asian man sitting behind the wheel. They exchange smiles, and I would really rather not be part of whatever he is doing. Hunting for sex or blood, or I don't know what.

The air tastes different in the city. At that house it tasted of dust and stone inside, and sweet jasmine and the perfume from the climbing roses in the garden. But here there's smog and a dash of salt spray from the distant Pacific Ocean. It has a definite aftertaste. As do the people nearby.

I turn away before I can fixate on the sight of all that blood rushing beneath their skin. Hunger will not control me. I am not an animal, no matter what he's done to me. The light turns green and away we go.

"What are the rules for being a vampire?" I ask.

"Do as I say."

*As if.*

It's truly ridiculous how attractive he is, with his flawless skin, deep blue eyes, and glossy, thick hair. The driver's-side window is down, and a breeze tousles his locks. He's like something out of an ad for cologne or designer jeans. Though, I guess that helps them ensnare the next meal.

His gaze is constantly on the move. Taking in the people on the sidewalks, other vehicles on the road, and the buildings we're passing. High-rises amaze him, and the digital advertising billboards fascinate him to no end. Along with a group of scantily clad people spilling out of a bar. And following close behind them is a woman who absolutely cannot be human.

"That woman," I say in horror. "She had amber eyes, and her teeth...holy shit!"

"Sounds like a werewolf," he says. "Such things have always been here. You're no longer susceptible to the human unwillingness to see what's in front of you. To excuse away the things that scare you. Don't be so shocked. What you consider unnatural is really just the parts of our world you have yet to experience."

None of this makes me happy. "So, what do you want at my work?"

"I haven't decided yet. But it's interesting that they had the house keys." He runs his tongue over his fangs as he looks people over as we drive. "The style of clothing has certainly changed."

"Your suit is dated. But people wear all sorts of things now. Dressing in vintage clothing is common enough."

He nods.

"Have you ever even seen a TV?"

"Yes. I bought my first one at the 1939 World's Fair." He points toward the circular Capitol Records Building. "They'd only just started work on that the last time I saw it."

"How old are you exactly?"

"Have I mentioned that your manners are appalling?"

"You attacked me, drank my blood, and turned me into a vampire. Do you really want to discuss manners?"

"Drinking blood is a matter of survival," he says. "I won't apologize for it. And I could have left you to rot. I still might."

Here's the thing. The idea of becoming a vampire is seductive, in theory. Movies make it look so good. Live forever and all that. But the actual process of being attacked and exsanguinated is traumatic as fuck. Not to mention all of the changes to your body. The demand that you leave your everyday life behind and embrace...whatever this is.

I press my hand to my chest, waiting to feel the beat of my heart. It doesn't happen. I hold my breath and wait. And wait some more.

"You don't need to breathe," he says. "You're just doing it out of habit."

"How were we even invented? Who made the first vampire?"

"Invented?" He laughs. "You make us sound like Frankenstein's monster. The truth is, no one knows for sure. Or no one I've ever met. I believe it's some sort of magic, though the how and why of it are lost to time."

"Magic is real?"

"Your heart no longer beats and yet you're still walking around. What would you call it?"

He has a point. Not that I'm going to admit that. "You haven't told me your name."

"Lucas."

"Lucas. Okay. I don't sparkle in sunlight now, do I?"

"No. You burn to ash." His dark brows draw together. "Sparkling. What an absurd idea. Why on earth would you think that?"

"No reason." My stomach churns. Good to know that even the undead experience anxiety. "Take the next left and park anywhere."

"We can't shapeshift, and nor can we control animals," he says in a truly testy voice. "I should have beat the shit out of Stoker when I had the chance. Same goes for Polidori and Le Fanu for breaking confidences and spinning such fantastical fallacies about our kind."

"Wait a minute. Are you talking about Bram Stoker? The guy who wrote *Dracula*? You actually knew him?"

"No," he answers eventually. "He was a friend of...never mind."

The Thorn Group owns an old, six-story building. Though what counts as old is debatable, given my current company. Imagine having beef with someone dating back centuries.

A security guard watches as I carefully swipe my card, and the glass doors slide open. He has white skin and military-short hair. And the bulk of his attention is on the man behind me in the vintage suit. The one who is staring at the sliding doors with an awestruck expression. Guess he hasn't seen those before either.

It can't really have only been a few hours ago that I walked out these doors. I wince at all of the bright lights. No wonder Lucas sticks to candles. It's your standard lobby, with a security desk and couple of elevators at the back. There's a couple of potted plants and a piece of modern art to give the space character. Keeping with tonight's theme, the artwork largely consists of red splashes of paint.

A delicious scent hits me as soon as I step foot inside, and my mouth begins to water. I can smell the man's blood, warm and fragrant. I can hear the way it whooshes through his veins and the steady beat of his heart. It calls to me like nothing I have ever known.

Lucas stands with his hand wrapped around the security guard's neck. I didn't even see him move. Then he stares into the man's eyes and asks, "Who owns this place?"

"Miss Cole," the security guard answers mechanically. He's not even struggling. Lucas has put him under some sort of compulsion. "She's working late tonight. Her office is on the top floor."

"Thank you." Lucas gestures me closer. "Come here, Skye. You need to feed."

"No. Absolutely not."

"It wasn't a question."

"You don't understand. Even if I could do that, there are security cameras watching us."

"Security cameras?"

"Yes." Then I remind myself he's ancient. "Like motion picture film cameras. But smaller. And they're pretty much everywhere when it comes to public spaces."

"What a horrifying development." He frowns and gazes around the room. "Can the cameras be turned off?"

"Yes, sir." The security guard nods. "Or the recording can be deleted. I'd be happy to do it for you."

"I appreciate that. Come here, Skye. Don't make me ask again."

My whole body is shaking with need.

"If you don't feed, you'll die," says Lucas. "That's certainly a choice you could make. But you need to know it won't happen straight away. Desiccation takes a while, even for a newborn. First the hunger will take control of you. We're standing in the middle of a city. Can you imagine the carnage you would cause?"

"You'd let that happen?"

He just sighs. "The last thing I need is attention from the human press or authorities. Doing it now, with me here, is your best chance of not killing anyone. I'm stronger than you, I can overpower you if necessary. Or just compel you to behave."

"Promise me you won't let me kill anyone."

After a moment, he nods. "Walk slowly over here."

The elevator chimes and a beautiful Black woman in a suit rushes out. "Wait! Don't hurt him. I have bags of donated blood."

"You look just like your grandmother," says Lucas with a smile.

"Mister Thorn. What a surprise."

"Apparently not."

He releases the security guard and takes a bag of blood from her. His nose wrinkles in distaste. "Donated blood, did you say?" He bites the end of the attached tube and sucks some down. "That's disgusting. It's cold and you can taste the plastic."

I've met Helena Cole on numerous occasions. Christmas parties and such. She's tall with natural hair, and her wardrobe is to die for. All of the best designers and shoes I would kill for. But all I can see and hear and smell right now is her blood. All I can focus on is how fast her heart is beating, and the vein raised just so in the side of her neck.

I don't remember making the decision. I just know that I am going to drink her dry. The realization crosses her face, and out of her coat pocket, she pulls a gun. Smart of her. Though it doesn't slow me down in the least. I am past the point of rational thought.

My body surges forward, hands reaching, ready to grab her—until I slam back into Lucas. One of his arms wraps around me, holding my arms against my body, and the tube on the bag of donated blood is pushed between my lips.

"Drink," he orders.

And I gratefully do as told.

"When you asked my grandmother to see to your estate during your absence, she took the task to heart." Helena Cole sits behind her large desk, the picture of composure. Though, she watches us both warily, and I doubt her gun has gone far. Which is honestly fair enough. "Not only overseeing your assets, but also investing a sizeable portion and growing it into what has now become The Thorn Group."

"I always liked Shirley." Lucas sits beside me with his legs crossed. He keeps casting the computer and landline phone curious glances. Any new technology seems to be of great interest to him. "I'm sorry to hear she passed."

"Thank you. She remembered you fondly and often."

I sit in the corner of the sofa with my third blood juice box. There's a fridge hidden in Helena's office with a handy supply for emergencies. While cold blood isn't the best thing I have ever tasted, it satiates my hunger. And that's the important thing. Now that I can think clearly, my behavior downstairs horrifies me. There was no me in the moment. No sign of morals or humanity. Only the hunger. That absolutely cannot happen again. "She worked for you?"

"When it suited her," he says. "I left her with enough money to do as she liked. But it doesn't surprise me that she built all this. She had a keen mind and a strong heart. She also got bored easily and was always searching for the next challenge."

The word *daughter* appears in my mind, surrounded by that strange stillness again. But I keep it to myself. It might just be my imagination. Given recent events, however, it might be more like weird, psychic powers. Asking Lucas for answers hasn't gone well so far, so I keep my mouth shut and listen.

A black-and-white photo hangs on the wall. Lucas and a little girl stand beside the piano in the house I was just at in The Hills. Judging by the style of clothing, it was probably taken sometime mid-last century. No wonder he considered Shirley family, if he knew her from when she was a child. Alongside that photo are a variety of framed degrees awarded to Helena.

"Managing director," says Lucas, reading from the plaque on the desk. "Society has come a long way."

"With regards to some things. But there's always more progress to be made. My grandmother wrote the rules for dealing with you and your property," says Helena in a no-nonsense tone of voice. "Inspections of your house have been carried out periodically over the past seventy years while you've been asleep. Any necessary maintenance was carried out only during daylight hours. You were never meant to be disturbed. What went wrong?"

Two sets of eyes turn to me expectantly. Awkward. "Everything was fine until I went into the basement."

"You entered the basement?"

"Yes."

Her lips thin in displeasure. "Jen didn't instruct you to stay out of that part of the house?"

"No. She didn't. The job was also given to me late in the afternoon. There was nothing mentioned about not being there at night."

"I see," says Helena, her hands clasped on the desk. With the way her eyes instantly hardened, I doubt my boss will have a job for long. "Mister Thorn's decisions are, of course, his own, but I apologize for the part The Thorn Group played in this. You were a member of our staff and…well."

The smirk returns to Lucas's face. "I think Helena is trying to apologize to you for me making you a vampire."

Before I can say anything, she withdraws an envelope from a drawer and announces, "I often wondered what I would do if this night ever came. Hand over your money and sever the connection, or carry on protecting you and your interests, as my grandmother wanted."

Lucas watches and waits with preternatural stillness.

"Complicating my decision-making on this was that my grandmother warned me of your kind's powers of compulsion. Meaning that if we were ever to meet, there would be a possibility that I would be henceforth robbed of my freewill." She takes a deep breath. "My grandmother believed you never used such an ability on her, and it's my hope and expectation that you will grant me the same respect."

"Of course," says Lucas.

Helena turns to me.

"We can really do that?"

"Yes," answers Lucas. "But it's no simple thing. It takes time to master the technique."

"Huh. I won't use it on you," I tell her.

Helena nods. "Lucas, she said you saved her from one of your own kind. That none of us would be here if you hadn't intervened. Therefore, I have to believe there is some good in you, despite what you've done to this woman."

"You are, of course, free to believe what you like, Miss Cole."

"She made me promise on her deathbed. There she lay with her family gathered around, and yet some of her last thoughts were of you."

Lucas says nothing.

"The Thorn Group has done a lot of good over the years. My grandmother insisted that a portion of your money be used to help people. Nothing she could do, however, would even begin to compensate for the deaths you left in your wake. But my grandmother also said, it's better the devil you know. And she knew things. She continued to talk to others of your kind once you were gone. It drove my mother wild that she put herself in danger like that. I am going to keep my word and trust that my grandmother knew what she was doing. For now."

Helena holds up a black credit card. "You can access your funds with this. Let me know what else you require. The head of our legal department is also a family member and is aware of your unique situation. He should be able to assist with anything that may arise."

"Anything?" asks Lucas, cocking his head.

"Within reason," says Helena in a flat and unfriendly tone. "We won't help you bury any bodies."

"I'd appreciate it if the house could be seen to."

"It'll be taken care of," says Helena. "Items my grandmother believed would be of use or interest to you have also been collected over the years. They'll be delivered tomorrow."

He nods.

"I must insist that there be no further mishaps involving my staff. And know that they will only visit the house during daylight hours."

"Understood."

"Skye, you will, of course, be compensated, since this happened to you while carrying out Thorn Group business."

I nod.

"Was that everything you required for now?"

"Yes," says Lucas. "Thank you."

"Please remember to compel the security guard into forgetfulness on your way out. It would be for the best if he never remembers you being here." Helena sits back in her chair. "Good night, Mister Thorn."

In the elevator heading down to the lobby, Lucas turns to me and says, "There aren't people who operate the elevator anymore?"

"No. You just press the button you need. It's pretty straightforward."

He nods. "I thought that meeting went quite well."

"She hates you."

"There seems to be a lot of that tonight."

"I mean, she really hates you, and she was not hiding it," I say. "I half expected you to throw a hissy fit."

He raises his eyebrows. "A hissy fit?"

"Yes. It means—"

"I can guess what it means." Another thing he does exceedingly well: sneering. "I do not throw hissy fits."

"Whatever you say." I inspect my nails. Even they seem stronger and brighter. "Can I really not go home?"

"When I was first turned, I was a lot like you. I missed my home and wanted to see my family. I thought I could control myself, control the hunger. There was a village nearby, so I tested myself. No one was left alive come dawn."

He gets all up in my face, backing me into the corner of the elevator, flashing his fangs. It's more than a little scary. When he speaks again, the words are laced with a European accent.

"What do you say, Skye, still want to go home?"

"No."

"No," he agrees. "I didn't think so."

"If you hadn't been there earlier, I would have killed her."

"Is that your way of saying thank you?"

"Of course, if you hadn't turned me, none of this would have happened in the first place."

He clicks his tongue impatiently.

When the elevator doors slide open, it is to a scene of slaughter. Blood is smeared across the gray marble floor of the lobby and halfway up the wall. The security guard's throat is torn open, his sightless eyes are staring at the ceiling.

A scream catches in my throat, and I slap my hands over my mouth to hold it inside.

Standing over the body, licking his fingers clean, is a young man with olive skin and long brown hair. Handsome, of course. And exceedingly tall and built. He is basically a murderous, bloodsucking lump of muscle.

"Christos," says Lucas. "Fancy seeing you here."

"You were followed. We had someone watching your house."

"For seventy years?"

The stranger's smile is purely predatory. "He wants to see you."

"Does he?" Lucas steps out of the elevator. "What a mess. Was killing him absolutely necessary?"

"I was hungry." Christos shrugs. "Who's the girl? Is she a newborn? Did you make her?"

"None of your concern."

His gaze narrows on me in a way that creeps me right the fuck out. The word *death* appears in my mind as I follow Lucas into the lobby. If this is a psychic gift compliments of the change, it could be more helpful. Because there's a whole lot of death happening around me. The poor security guard. And still, it's all I can do not to drop to the floor and start licking up his blood. Such a heady scent. It's delicious. My hands start shaking, and holding myself back is not easy. Thank fuck I filled up on the blood bags upstairs.

"Was that all you were asked to tell me?" asks Lucas. "That he wishes me to pay him a visit?"

A scowl twists Christos's face, and his huge hands curl into fists. "It's an order, not an invitation."

Lucas nods and smiles.

"Look at you. You look like shit." The other vampire laughs mockingly. "My how the mighty have fallen."

Despite my heightened senses, I can barely track Lucas when he moves. He is little more than a blur. But suddenly he's standing beside the other vampire, his hand stained red, and in it there's a...oh fucking hell. It's his heart.

Christos folds to the floor, his chest a bloody ruin. He didn't have time to react to the attack. Lucas was just that damn fast. The male's remains lie there for no more than a moment before his body turns into a pile of ash.

"Holy shit," I mutter, stunned.

Lucas pulls a handkerchief out of his coat pocket and proceeds to wipe the ash from his hand. No other trace of the vampire remains. I'm not sure what shocked me more. The quick and brutal murder, or the pile of ash that's all that remains of his body. Both, probably.

And with the way information is flooding my mind, it is hard to know what to freak out about first. Me wanting to lick blood off the floor. Lucas displaying superpowers. Or the way my whole life has hit the wall and gone splat. He's already threatened to make me deader. Will he rip my heart out, too, if I displease him?

"You killed him," I say, just making conversation. "Tore out his heart."

Lucas tucks the handkerchief away. "Yes."

"I, um, I think I'm going to be sick."

His expression turns pained. "Vampires do not get nausea, Skye. We certainly do not vomit. Would you please show some decorum?"

My gaze is drawn back to the blood, and the dead body of the security guard, and the piles of ash that was Christos...and oh man. "Why did you kill him? Was it because of the guard?"

"Partly because he followed me here and killed the security guard. The guard was an employee of Thorn Group, and therefore, should be considered under my protection. And such reckless killing cannot be encouraged. But mostly because he was disrespectful."

"He was so much bigger than you, but you just..."

"Yes." His mouth skews with amusement. "Strength isn't always about size."

I frown as I consider his words. "Helena is not going to be happy."

"There's little I can do about that right now. This is one body The Thorn Group is going to have to bury. Because we have somewhere we need to be."

# CHAPTER THREE

The Boulevard Hotel is one of the oldest-running establishments in Hollywood. Though, its glamor days are long gone. There's more than a faint air of disrepair in the worn carpet and faded wallpaper. A woman is busy on her cell behind the reception desk. She doesn't even spare us a glance as we make our way toward the bank of elevators. There are no guests hanging out in the lobby. Given it's nearing midnight, most normal people must be in bed.

I should be home asleep by now. Not that there's anyone to miss me. It's been a while since I shared my life with a special someone (besides myself, of course). Since Jason broke my heart and dumped me for a thinner version of me who had more of an upward career trajectory. And you can bet he told me all of this to my face. What a dick.

But prior to this evening, lousy exes were the sort of thing topping my list of woes. Along with other ordinary everyday details. Like figuring out how to both pay for new tires and my rent. How painfully mundane. Attacking people to drink their blood didn't even rate a mention.

Lucas ushers me into an elevator, inspects the control panel, and presses a button for a subbasement level.

The lowest you can go. A small smile curves his lips at the accomplishment. Which would be cute if he wasn't a complete psychopath. "Stay close and keep your mouth shut. The family that runs this place is not our friend."

The death of the security guard and removal of Christos's heart has shocked me into submission. For the moment, at least. No amount of violent television or film prepared me for actually seeing a dead body and witnessing someone's death. Or second death. Lucas didn't even hesitate about killing him. This world I have entered is really a lot.

I stare at my reflection in the mirrored elevator wall. Yay that I have a reflection. Boo that it takes me a moment to recognize myself. My skin has taken on the same flawless sheen as my maker's. To think of all the skincare products I've used to try and achieve exactly this. My dirty-blonde hair is now supermodel levels of thick and lustrous. But it's my eyes that are truly creepy. The usual, confused color combination has changed to a clear pale green.

I might have been forgettable before, but now I am officially hot and utterly unnatural. You would have to be a fool to think there wasn't something going on with me. Especially given the teeth. I grimace at my reflection, and two long canines are plainly visible, brutally sharp and shining white.

"We stay the same as when we died," he says. "Only prettier. It helps to lure in prey. Normal humans don't tend to notice our eyes or teeth."

"How do they not see it?"

"That we're predators?" he asks with a sly smile. "I always thought it was partly a kind of magic, but it's partly also that they don't want to see it. Never doubt the power of denial. Their safe little worlds don't have room for the likes of us. How would they sleep at night if they knew there really were monsters hiding in the dark?"

Nice to see no blood or dead body on the floor when the elevator doors open this time. We step into a boring concrete corridor, where a man wearing a neat black suit stands waiting. He has white skin and a shaved head and pointy teeth. Not a man then, a vampire. Like Christos, he is seriously tall and built. Larger even than my companion, who has to be bordering on six-and-a-half feet tall. And behind this new, oversized dude is a large, steel door. The sort that belongs to a refrigerator unit.

"Sir," he says in a deep voice.

"Berin." Lucas smiles. "It's good to see you. I believe he's waiting for me?"

The giant says no more. He bows his head and holds the door open for us. He does, however, give me serious side-eye. No idea what that's about.

Inside, there's a party happening. The crowded space is a speakeasy. A beautiful Art Deco bar in decline. With worn, green velvet couches, palms scattered around, and dusty pendant lighting. There's a wall of liquor bottles and a stage and dance floor. The customers range from couples in formal wear out of a bygone era to what resembles a motorcycle club in the corner. So much leather.

I'm not sure my cottage-core aesthetic holds up to this lifestyle. No one else here is wearing anything like my gray cardigan, blue floral dress, navy tights, and flat ankle boots.

From what I can see, they all have sharp teeth.

Hold that thought. A waitress flirting with a patron at the bar is actually human.

Music is pouring out of the sound system, the bass loud enough to vibrate through my chest. But I can still hear the way the waitress's blood is pumping through her body. Like my whole being is focused on this one need. The need to feed.

My hands start shaking and my mouth waters. Thankfully, I'm still not hungry enough to attack. Not yet. But the thirst is there, coiled inside me, waiting to pounce. This sucks. Can I really do this? Be one of the bloodsucking undead? Given the only other option is true death, and that doesn't exactly appeal...

The human waitress's date casually leans in and bites her neck. And with a beatific grin, she closes her eyes and succumbs to the moment. All I can do is watch.

Lucas walks back to me impatiently. "What are you staring at?"

I nod at the couple by the bar.

"It is possible to find willing victims. Some of them even like it. Come on." He grabs my hand and leads me toward a door at the back of the bar.

The weight of the stares of those we pass becomes heavier with each step. No one tries to stop us or talk to us, but they all whisper and watch. I have never been in a roomful of killers. Not to my knowledge, at least. And their uncanny beauty and grace is disturbing.

I hold on to his hand as tight as I can. Guess Shirley was right, better the devil you know.

Another ridiculously tall and built vampire guards the door at the back of the room. It's like someone made an army of undead himbos. This one nods to Lucas and steps aside. No one seems to be making a move, so I reach out to open the door. And the handle promptly breaks and comes off in my hand. Oops.

Lucas swears under his breath.

"Sorry," I say. "I was trying to be careful."

He snatches the handle from me and gives it to the guard, who is now looking at me with a mildly horrified expression. Damaging the fittings is obviously a major faux pas. Lucas pushes the door open and drags me inside. And he says *my* manners are appalling.

There are no Art Deco touches in here. The spacious back room is painted black and is bare apart from a myriad of thick white candles and a long wooden table with five, throne-like chairs behind it. Vampires are seated in three of the chairs. And the only other creature in the room is one standing off to the side, wearing a long black robe and holding a digital notebook and stylus. Guess he's here to take notes. A supernatural, undead personal assistant. Ha.

Lucas pulls his hand out of my grip, steps forward, and says, "You wished to see me?"

"Hello, Lucas." A stunning woman with umber skin and her long hair in braids gives him a smile. Her blood-red dress dips low at the front to reveal a massive ruby pendant. A definite statement piece. "It's been a while."

"Rose."

"Where is Christos?" demands an old man. He looks ancient, with white skin and hair. The style of his suit is dated as heck. Something from a century or more ago meant for hanging out in ballrooms or carriages. "He was supposed to accompany you."

"My apologies, Archie," says Lucas. "He won't be joining us."

He snarls. "You killed him?"

"Yes."

"He was mine." His lips flatline. "You had no right."

"Have I really been gone so long that you thought I would tolerate being followed?" asks Lucas. "Let alone his disrespectful behavior. He killed one of my lackeys."

"Never did know when to keep his mouth shut," says the last person at the table, a handsome man with brown skin and dark hair. "But you can't go around just killing our kind, Lucas. At least, not ones from other families without the agreement of their sire or the board. We have rules now."

"What rules, Javier?" asks Lucas with a raised brow. "There's a board?"

"You've been gone a while. Seventy years. Much has changed." Rose taps her nails against the table. She nods to the man writing on his digital notepad in the corner. "The scribe will ensure a copy of the rules are sent to you if you give him your email."

Lucas turns to me with one dark brow raised in question.

"Your electronic mail address," I say. "We can set one up later."

"The point is, we rule Los Angeles now," growls Archie. "Not you."

Rose clears her throat. "Things got a little out of hand near the end of the last century. A group of younger ones started running wild and causing chaos. Leaving bodies lying around for humans to find. Far more than their officials could reasonably be expected to ignore or excuse. They put our whole race at risk."

"I see," says Lucas.

"This board was formed, and one of our first decisions was to implement a cull. The troublemakers were destroyed, along with any known to associate with them. Many lives were lost in the conflict, but it was necessary."

"It was the only way for us to regain control," says Archie.

"We had no choice. They were making swarms of newborns to aid them in their stupidity," says Javier. "The seventies were a trial, but the nineties were a fucking mess. We came this close to all-out war. You're lucky you missed it. Though, the music was quite good."

"Once it was done, we did our best to put the violence behind us. The board started to meet regularly to discuss any issues regarding our kind. We have as little as possible to do with the human world. They're more than capable of governing themselves. But the board agreed to adhere to a set of rules for a term of thirty years to avoid another cull," says Rose. "One of these rules was a moratorium on creating newborns."

"Which is still in effect until we vote on it in a few days, unfortunately," says Archie, turning his hateful gaze to me. "Awful timing on your part. This one will, therefore, have to be destroyed."

I freeze in horror. They want to kill me, and Lucas doesn't say a damn thing. We may have only known each other a few hours, but surely I am owed a little loyalty?

Rose frowns. "He was unaware of the rule when he made her."

"Ignorantia juris non excusat. Ignorance of the law is no excuse." Archie slams the table with the flat of his hand, making the thick wood groan. "I'll do it myself if you lack the conviction. And I'll do it slowly. It'll be a fitting punishment for him killing my guard."

"You're about to vote on these things?" asks Lucas, ignoring the other man's tantrum. "How were the board members chosen?"

"Some of the rules will perhaps be eased. And isn't it obvious?" Javier shrugs. "We're the strongest and our families the largest."

Lucas nods. "Who owns The Hills?"

"I do," says Archie. "Central L.A. is mine. You've rested on my lands for decades."

"The runes must have really bothered you." Lucas slips his hands into his pants pockets. "Not being able to step foot on my property."

"I'll break them one day, Lucas. That, I promise. And when I do, I'm coming for your head."

"Not in the next few days without our approval, you're not," says Javier. "I am sorry, Lucas, but we cannot let your newborn live. We've gone almost thirty years with no exceptions. We can't afford to look weak now."

And again, Lucas says nothing. The fucker.

"Wait." I rush forward. "You can't just kill me. Again."

Lucas grabs my arm and holds me back. "Quiet, Skye. Why divvy up the city, Rose?"

"To enable us to enforce the rules. It was either divide the city and give the strongest families the job of patrolling the territory or form some sort of central army. The first option was the fastest to implement and seemed the best idea at the time."

Behind us, the broken door opens and the big dude enters. The one who had been standing guard. He tries to shut the door behind him, the broken handle stopping him. Music from the bar floats through, and oh man. I swear the monster's footsteps shake the room, he's so damn huge. And he's coming straight for me. There's no emotion displayed on his face. It's impossible to know if he cares about turning me to ash or not.

"Say goodbye to your sire," says Archie, with his trademark evil grin.

"Fuck you," I say.

"Language." Lucas sighs. "It would seem this is unfortunately inevitable."

"It's nothing personal," agrees Javier "You can see we have no choice. The rules have kept peace in the city for decades now."

"What happens if they're set aside?"

"They won't be. Not all at once. That would be chaos. But an easing of some of them will allow the vampires in the area to return to being largely self- or family-governed."

"Interesting," says the jerk who turned me.

"Lucas," I hiss. "Do something!"

Like the utter bastard he is, he simply pats me on the hand. All I can do is stare in disbelief. He is absolutely going to just stand there and let me die. I don't believe this shit.

Then, in a blur, he flies at the large vampire and separates his head from his neck.

It's as if Lucas's hands turned into claws or something. Or they're just that damn strong. I have no idea why he's more powerful. But thank goodness he is. Blood sprays everywhere, and the body falls with a thump before it turns to ash. The air around us fills with gray dust.

Rose just sighs.

Archie screeches and rises from his seat, but Lucas isn't finished. He leaps across the table and attacks him, too. Both of their bodies blur as they fight, Archie's hands beating at Lucas's chest.

Then Lucas decapitates him, as well. It's a lot messier than his heart extraction. Acid burns the back of my throat, but I swallow it down. Neither Rose nor Javier seems impressed with this turn of events. Neither of them moves to intervene, however. I back up until my spine hits the wall, my eyes as wide as the moon. Vampire politics are something else.

Kneeling on the long wooden table, Lucas pulls out his handkerchief for the second time tonight and wipes off his hands. Though with the amount of ash covering him, it's a wasted effort.

Rose slumps back in her seat. "Archie shouldn't have threatened you. That was foolish."

"Most people feel better after a nap," says Javier. "But you seem to have woken up in an even fouler mood than before."

"We can make a case for him having challenged you, which resulted in this." Rose frowns. "But you can't just go around killing vampires. Especially not board members. We really do have rules now. At least for the next few days."

"Don't make us have to hunt you."

Lucas' smile is bitter. "I can't believe you want to regulate our existence. Attempting to avoid just that is why most of us came here."

"It was necessary," says Rose. "You have no idea the dangers we faced."

"Do you truly believe either of us would have agreed to it otherwise?" asks Javier.

Lucas grunts. "No one touches a hair on my pretty little newborn's head."

Rose sighs some more. "Yes. You've made that quite clear."

"The Hills are mine." Lucas jumps off the table. "I don't want to see another vampire in the area uninvited."

"We'll see that word gets around," says Rose. "But Archie's family is sizeable, and their loyalty to him zealous, to say the least. I would anticipate visitors out for revenge, if I were you. Whether we condone such activities or not."

Lucas nods. "I understand."

"You are, of course, permitted to defend yourself. Will you be taking Archie's seat on the board?"

"Hell no."

"Lucas." Rose sighs. "One way or another, someone will need to represent your territory. Even if the rules are relaxed, we hope to continue working together for the betterment of our kind."

"I am not spending the rest of eternity in fucking board meetings." He wanders over to stand at my side. His vintage suit is trashed. The formerly white shirt smudged with ash. "It was good to see you both. Hopefully next time we can have a proper visit and not talk business."

Javier just waves him away.

"You picked the worst damn time to wake up. It would have been simpler if you'd stayed asleep," says Rose. "You know that, don't you?"

"I know," says Lucas. "But it was time. Or near enough."

"Time for what?" I ask as we're heading out the door. I do my best to keep any lingering fear out of my voice. And any hint of a freak-out off my face. Lucas doesn't seem the type to appreciate either.

The trip back through the bar is even worse this time. Patrons are no longer content with just whispers and stares. We're actually getting growled at. Which is rude. In all likelihood, they're members of Archie's family.

"Time to live, Skye," he says, throwing an arm around my shoulders. As if his night of killing has made him merry. Such a psychopath. "It's time for us to live."

## CHAPTER FOUR

Behind the scarred door in the basement of the house in the Hollywood Hills is a network of rooms. It's a little like Batman's lair, but with fewer bats and no technology. It's actually quite homey, with paintings, black-and-white photos, and tapestries on the walls. And all of the furniture is antique; there's even a chandelier.

The door opens into a sprawling, grandiose living room with a collection of Chesterfields, chaise lounges, and wingbacks. There's also a long wooden table that seats twelve. A wall of books that appear to be even older than the ones upstairs, and several cabinets full of curiosities. A wide hallway leads off from the room. That's where the bedroom is, along with a variety of other locked doors.

Lucas heads through his bedroom and into the attached bathroom upon our return, with me following close behind. We didn't talk much on the drive back to the house. I think I was in shock. But now I have questions, and lots of them. As much as I resent Lucas, he is my sole teacher when it comes to the undead and this new life of mine.

"Are the heart and the head the main ways to kill vampires?" I ask.

"Yes," he says, shrugging out of his filthy suit jacket and toeing off his shoes. "Plotting my downfall already?"

"A girl needs her hobbies."

He snorts. "Hold on to your sense of humor, Skye. It'll serve you well in the centuries to come. Fire and sunlight can also kill, but you need sustained exposure."

"I don't suppose you have any magical rings that enable us to walk around in daylight?"

He stares blankly at me.

"Just asking."

"A talisman like that might well be possible, but it would take a lot of power to create. I've never met a witch who liked me that much, or one who was that powerful."

"Shocking that they wouldn't like you." My head is a mess of thoughts and feelings. It really has been a hell of a night. "You mentioned runes back at that vampire bar."

"A druid I knew needed some fast cash and agreed to work on this place when it was being built. He etched runes into the stone walls down here to protect and keep. Think of it as casting a spell."

The bathroom is immaculate black and white, with cool fixtures straight out of the 1920s. In particular, a big, old clawfoot bathtub looks inviting. The shower is suspended over it with a curtain to keep the water from splashing onto the floor.

"There are druids too?" I ask, my brows raised. "The protect part I understand, but what does keep do?"

"This world is bigger than you know. Much more than humans and animals walk the Earth. As for the runes, look around." He gestures about us. "Notice how these rooms aren't as stale and dusty as you'd expect after being closed up for seventy years?"

"The ones aboveground are, though."

"I usually have staff to deal with upstairs. The runes are concentrated down here in my real home."

"And I was the first person to disturb you in seventy years?"

"You, Skye, either ignore your instincts or have a very strong will," he says.

Neither sounds like a compliment.

"As far as humans are concerned, the protection tends to discourage the curious and dissuade thieves. The runes will only outright stop another preternatural creature without an invitation. That's enough questions. Go away now."

"Just a few more."

"It's been a long first night back. Don't make me decapitate you, too."

"Pretty please?"

He groans and starts unbuttoning his shirt. "What else?"

"They said you used to rule L.A.? What are you, like the vampire king or something?"

He snorts. "No. There is no vampire king in this country. I never ruled L.A. I was simply the strongest in the city for a time. Perhaps I still am. I don't know."

"Have you made vampires before, and if so, where are they now?"

"Not here," he says. "Though, at least, one of them should be."

"Can we still eat and drink human food?"

"Why would you want to?"

"Because donuts. Duh. But hang on, you have all of that wine out there."

"I like the scent."

"How were you able to kill Archie?" I ask, leaning against the doorframe. "For someone so important, he was dispatched pretty easily."

"Strength comes with age. I am older and, therefore, stronger. The strength of the one who turned you can also play a part."

Off comes his shirt, and wow, that's a lot of muscles for one man. The old suit was doing him a serious disservice.

His shoulders and chest have definition for days. It must have been a while since I saw a man half naked, because not staring at him is harder than it should be. Not that he is the least bit aware of me ogling him. Me and my issues aren't even on his radar.

"Archie was only turned around 1850. But he was tenacious. Killed his sire early and started building himself a coterie of guards. If he hadn't gone for size and scariness over actual fighting skills when he made them, they might have been able to defend him from me, and he might still be with us."

"He was a hundred and seventy?"

"Rose is about eight hundred, and Javier was turned when this country was colonized."

My eyes are as wide as the moon. "Huh."

He undoes the button and zipper on his pants and pushes both them and his boxers to the ground. Nudity is obviously not an issue for him. I turn around before I can see it all. Though a fleeting glimpse suggests he's a man of size. Next, I hear the groaning of pipes and the sound of water falling. My hearing is sensitive enough to make out the soft splashes from his footfalls as he steps into the shower.

"The oldest vampires, ones born BC, haven't left their castles or caves in millennia. They have minions fetch their food," he says. "But not many of us manage to survive that long. Some simply lack the will. After a couple of centuries, time starts to lose meaning. Once you've seen and done it all, there doesn't always seem to be a reason to continue. But more practically, it's hard to remain hidden. We need humans to feed on, but they tend to get upset and hunt us once the bodies start piling up."

"You said we could feed without killing."

"We can. I didn't lie to you. It just takes practice and control. But some prefer to give in to their instincts and bleed victims dry. The rush from killing can be substantial. It'll be interesting to see what these new rules of theirs entail regarding such matters."

"Getting involved in vampire politics was not on my list of plans," I say. "What about drinking animal blood?"

"It's adequate, but the taste is subpar," he says. "Are you out of questions yet?"

The water and soap he's using smell nice. "I'm done for now. Oh. Where's my phone?"

"I left it with Helena. Did you know people can track you with those things?" he asks, sounding sort of amazed.

"When did you do that?"

"When we first got up to her office. You were busy feeding. She explained that keeping it would be a mistake."

"But I want to call my mom so she's not freaking out, wondering where I am. I've thought up a story that's plausible. I'll tell her work is sending me to a foreign office. Then I'll fake some pictures of me in France or something. I have it all planned out. I don't know if I can do this...be like you. But I am not ready to die again yet, either."

Nothing from him.

"Do you think the security guard had family?"

"Helena will ensure they're taken care of," he says.

I rest my head against the doorframe and close my eyes. Just for a moment. My body is weary. My strength and vitality diminished. I still don't feel hungry, so I don't think it's due to lack of blood. However, my mind is mush.

"You're falling asleep on your feet," he says. "Go lie down."

"Guess it must be close to dawn. We sleep all day, right?"

"No," he says as the water turns off. "The older you get, the less sleep you need. But you're a newborn and still adapting. Your brain has been dealing with a rush of new information from your heightened senses. It needs time to rest. Go lie down. The bed's right there."

"I'm going to go lie down for a minute," I say, wandering off toward the bedroom.

"What a brilliant idea," the wet and naked vampire grumbles behind me.

"Father," singsongs someone in a loud and obnoxious voice.

I am lying on the four-poster bed with Lucas stretched out beside me, reading a book, apparently. It is an oddly domestic scene to wake up to. Guess he was enjoying either the book or the quiet, since he moans, "Give me strength."

He put a blanket on me at some stage. Nice of him. All I remember is being so tired that I face planted on the bed. It was a lot like how a friend's toddler operated. Go, go, go, stop.

"Is it sunset?" I ask in a sleepy voice.

Lucas nods. "Yes."

A tall, young man with lots of blond hair appears in the bedroom doorway and grins. His body is lean and his face all sharp edges. Kind of like a male model. And when he talks, he does so with an English accent. "Hello, old man."

"Henry. I wondered when you'd make an appearance."

"Who's this with you?" He bounces his butt on the end of the bed and studies me with interest. "Goodness, do you have all of the gossips abuzz. Word on the street is I have a new sibling. How exciting."

"Why are you asking if you already know who she is?" Lucas sits up and sets his book aside. He's wearing a pair of pajama pants and not much else. Not staring at his chest is a big ask.

"Because it annoys you."

Lucas grunts.

"I'm Henry." He offers me his hand to shake. "What's your name?"

"Skye. Hi."

"A blonde with green eyes. How interesting. I thought you swore off making any more of us," says Henry. "In fact, I distinctly remember you doing so."

"Has the house been seen to?" asks Lucas, ignoring the question.

"Yes." Henry uses his hold on my hand to pull me out of bed. "Now then, little sister. Let's get you cleaned up. We do have a family reputation to maintain, after all."

"She needs to eat first." Lucas leaves the room and returns with a blood bag in each hand. "The fridge has been stocked. Here. Hold it carefully. You don't want to break it."

"Thank you." I put the tube between my lips and start sipping.

"You're one of those, are you?" asks Henry. "I admit, blood bags are practical, but hardly a substitute for the real thing."

Lucas raises his dark brows. "I tried to tell her, but she's happy, so..."

"It really is grand to see you." Henry opens his arms. "How about a hug?"

"Don't make me kill you," says Lucas.

"Father's love language is death threats," whispers Henry. "Try not to take it personally. Very difficult childhood. Not even Freud could sort him out; though, he certainly tried for a good many years."

"Are there any other siblings?" I ask.

Lucas frowns. It must be his fallback setting. "None that we need to discuss right now."

"Father spent his first few hundred years as a spy and a thug. It makes him slow to trust," says Henry. He turns back to Lucas. "I had almost forgotten how repressed you are. You know us men are more in touch with our feelings now. We actually talk about things. Occasionally, we even cry. You should try it sometime."

Despite the pout on Henry's face, the word that appears in my mind is *joy*. He is beyond delighted at this reunion with his sire. And that these words are still coming to me consistently is interesting. I need all the help I can get in navigating this new world.

We adjourn to the living room, where Henry flops down onto a blue velvet couch. After putting an Ella Fitzgerald album on the antique phonograph, Lucas sits gracefully in a black wingback. The largest chair in the room. It kind of looks like a throne, which makes sense. I curl up in the corner of a black leather sofa. And yay me for not breaking anything yet tonight. All of the furniture seems sturdy. To guard against vampires who don't know their own strength, perhaps?

"I wasn't supposed to wake you for another almost thirty years," says Henry, curling a blond lock around a finger. "What happened?"

Lucas nods to me. "She happened."

"It was an accident," I say, setting aside my breakfast for the moment. "My boss forgot to tell me to stick to the aboveground levels and to only be here during daylight hours."

Henry sobers. "That must have been terrifying for you. Facing a starving vampire on your own. You're lucky it was Father, who has enough control to stop himself and generally doesn't drink to kill. Otherwise, you'd be dead as a dodo."

I wisely keep my mouth shut.

"No wonder you turned her," continues Henry. "You must have felt like absolute shit with that eternally tortured soul of yours."

Lucas frowns. "We're vampires, drinking people's blood is what we do."

"Well, yes, but there's no need to be rude about it. And, old man, even you have to admit that attacking someone like that and draining them is...ugh. Déclassé. You must have terrified her, all desiccated and dried up like you would have been."

"She's one woman," says Lucas. "You were in a frenzy for half of 1943 on the frontlines. You killed thousands."

"They were Nazis. They had it coming."

Lucas shakes his head. "Enough. I'm not having this damn conversation with you."

"Since you have Henry here to help you adapt to this new age, do you still need me, or am I free to go?" I ask, sounding far braver than I feel.

Lucas's gaze turns hard. "And where exactly would you go?"

"Sweetie," says Henry. "Trust me when I tell you, you don't want to be alone out there on your own. Not right now. In a couple of days they'll probably be relaxing the rules, and no one is quite sure what's going to happen. It's been like living in a dictatorship, being here for the last thirty years. Having to watch over your shoulder for the board's bogeymen all the time. But is tyranny truly any better than anarchy? I suspect we're about to find out."

"We can discuss it later," says Lucas. "Henry, why are there rips in your clothes? Did you run out of money?"

Henry gasps. "Excuse you. These jeans are designer. I invested in Apple in the late seventies and made millions."

"You invested in fruit?" asks Lucas.

"Computers, Father. Apple computers. Please try to keep up!"

I sip my blood and stay silent.

"So, spill the tea. What was all of that decapitating about last night?" asks Henry, crossing his legs and getting comfortable. "I've been living quietly in this city for decades, and now all of a sudden I'm back in the limelight because of you."

"I highly doubt that." He smooths his palm over the arm of the chair. "A show of strength was required."

Henry nods. "Archie has been salty about your GOAT status for years."

"Am I supposed to understand a word of what you just said?"

"GOAT means greatest of all time," I explain. "He's paying you a compliment."

Lucas looks toward heaven. Though, I doubt any of us are welcome there.

"This is so much fun," says Henry. "You should have made a Skye years ago. Not only is she decorative, but she keeps the peace. Having a sister like her is fantastic."

"I'm so glad you approve."

"What shall we do together first?" asks Henry. "Oh, I know, have you ever been to Paris?"

I set the empty blood bag aside. "I've never even been out of the country."

"Well, you're rich and immortal now. It's time to start thinking big," says Henry. "Where do you want to go first?"

"I'm rich?"

"Oh, yeah." He wiggles his eyebrows. "Not even taking into consideration all of the money Shirley made. That woman was a genius when it came to finances. Be it the stock market or properties...she ruled them all. But what do you think Father has in all of those wooden chests out there?"

"Bodies?"

"No. Though, that would be hilariously macabre." Henry laughs. "Father is almost as old as the hills and has plenty of wealth to share."

"Do I now?" asks Lucas.

"You've been hoarding gold long since before the first crusade."

"You're that old?" I ask with wonder.

"Older. But it's a sensitive subject. He doesn't like to talk about his age."

"Wealth is easy when you live for centuries on end," says Lucas. "You hold on to knickknacks or books or weapons for nostalgia. And before you know it, they're considered priceless relics. Human lives are so short, they're willing to pay anything to connect with their past."

"True enough." Henry carries on, "So, Skye, you'll probably want to hang around town until after your funeral. It's good to get your mortal life out of the way. Put it all behind you and make a clean start. We could take the private jet next weekend and head over to Europe for a while. It'll be great."

"Wait," I say. "What?"

"Since when do I own a private jet?" asks Lucas, talking over the top of me.

"You don't, old man. But I do. These are the sort of advancements you miss out on when you decide to snooze for a century. And I know you had your reasons. But still... very dramatic of you, wouldn't you say?"

"Skye's not going anywhere."

"How possessive," says Henry in a teasing tone of voice. "It's not like you to be so territorial."

"She hasn't even adjusted to the change yet, you idiot. There's no way I am letting her go flying around the world with you."

My stomach, meanwhile, has sunk through the floor. "My funeral?"

"You hadn't heard?" asks Henry, doing the preternaturally still thing. His gaze jumps to Lucas then back to me. "There was a fire in your apartment last night. A body was found. You're officially dead, sweetie. Congratulations."

"What?" My mouth hangs open. "Did you know about this?"

"I knew Helena was going to do something," says Lucas. "Your vehicle has been taken as well. They would have been careful to make sure no one else was hurt in the fire and the body would have already been deceased. It's for the best."

"But my mom..." I don't know how I feel about this. Numb, mostly. So much has happened in such a short amount of time. "I'm really dead. That life is over."

"Yes," says Henry, in a somber tone of voice. Though, it doesn't last long. "You know what that means? It's time for your wake!"

## CHAPTER FIVE

While we hid from the sun, the aboveground floors had been transformed. There's no sign of the dust covers and everything is shiny. The scent of lemon cleanser fills the air. A large-screen TV has been hung in place of a painting in the living room, and there's plenty of blood bags for me in the fridge. Even the piano has been tuned, as demonstrated by Henry banging out "Moonlight Sonata." New cellphones and laptops wait on the dining room table.

Lucas, however, walks straight into the main bedroom on the upper floor and starts perusing the selection of modern clothing left for him.

"Shirley left instructions for a set of new suits to be made each year by that place you like on Saville Row. So you're all up to date. These are only a portion of them." Henry lounges on the king-size bed made up in charcoal-gray linens. "Let me tell you, the ones from the seventies were ugly as hell. Not even your precious tailors could salvage that decade. Shirl and I downed a bottle of Bollinger and burned them in her fireplace one night. We had a ball. However, you would have liked the punk era. Now *they* knew how to have fun."

"You were supposed to look after her," says Lucas, in a low voice.

"Father." Henry sighs. "She passed of old age in her own bed surrounded by a loving family. There was nothing to be done. Humans die. No matter how much we sometimes wish otherwise."

"She never changed her mind and asked you to turn her?"

"No. She remained wiser than all of us to the end."

Lucas stares at the clothes with a blank expression.

"Enough of this depressing nonsense." Henry jumps off the bed and grabs my hand. "Let's go see what they left for you, little sister. Helena keeps a personal shopper with excellent taste on staff. I should know, we were shagging for a while. Me and the shopper, that is. She used to adore me when she was a little girl, but Helena would probably now stake me on sight. Her mother's distaste for us was contagious, unfortunately."

Given he appears to be in his early twenties, and I am a solid thirty, being called his little sister is odd, to say the least. I follow him into the next bedroom, which is also freshly cleaned with the bed made. An armoire is bursting with clothing, shoes, and accessories. "Holy shit. Is this all for me?"

Henry smiles and starts rummaging through it all. "I love a good makeover."

"There's a lot of black."

"It's just practical. Newborns have a tendency to make a mess and spill their food. Black is the only color that hides blood."

It doesn't look like any of my actual belongings are here, though. "Did they burn everything I owned in the fire?"

"Helena would have wanted it to look authentic, I suspect," he says with a wince. "But I am sure she'll see to it that your family receives a hefty life insurance payout, if that helps."

"Money doesn't fix everything."

"No," he allows. "But take it from someone who grew up without any, it's better than the alternative."

I sit on the bed and take a moment to pull myself together. My parents must be devastated. At least they still have my brother. The thought that Christmas was our last time together as a family hurts. Especially since we argued about me staying in L.A. and I cut the trip short by a day. All of those precious moments we wasted.

We had been tentatively discussing a trip together to Hawaii later this year. Maybe that's what they'll do with the money, buy a place on the beach. Mom always dreamed of being closer to the ocean, and Dad would be able to fish to his heart's content.

My best friend, Nicole, will have to find someone else to be her bridesmaid. Someone else with whom to share secrets and bad jokes and two-in-the-morning drunken revelations. We were going to save our pennies and open a book shop together one day. Not that either of us were good with money, or even particularly liked dealing with other people. But we both loved romance books and hanging out together. It was a beautiful dream, and now it's gone.

"Why don't you go take a shower?" suggests Henry in a gentle tone. "Get that ash and muck off you and freshen up. You'll feel better."

"Yeah," I say with a discreet sniffle. "I think I will."


Vampires like a party, apparently. And Henry invited half of the undead in L.A. to the house. There are even real live humans in the mix, but they're all in the know. None of them bother to hide the bite marks on their bodies. Thankfully, my control is a little better tonight. Being freshly fed doesn't hurt. But I still have a bad habit of gawking at them. I am officially a creep. I don't mean to be. The blood calls to me and I forget myself. Which is probably why Henry sticks to my side like glue. To make sure I don't lose control again and attack anyone.

As he would say, déclassé.

Music by Olivia Rodrigo pumps out through the open windows and doors. Henry and I are in the back courtyard area off the dining and living rooms. Party lights have been strung from the pergola and the overgrown garden has been tamed. Even the water feature has been cleaned and filled. This vibe out here is nice.

I didn't last long inside. Too many voices and bodies and scents. Too many eyes staring at me. Anything new is a novelty to vampires, apparently. And I am the first newborn in a long time in this city. But yeah...inside the house was beyond overwhelming. My body is also being weird in new ways tonight. Like, I'm turned on for no reason. Even the brush of my clothes against my skin is enough to elicit a response. So strange. However, being outside in the night air is lovely.

What's truly amazing is the beauty of the world with my vampire sight. Guess I was dealing with too many things last night to be able to appreciate it. But the curve of a leaf or a petal on a flower can be dazzling. The distant lights of the city below hold me spellbound. And the ability to see the expanse of stars in the heavens shining above is amazing. There are no words.

"I worked for a gambling hall, running messages and helping in the stables," explains Henry when I ask for his origin story. "No real options beyond grunt work for a lowborn bastard. But I had a talent for card games and word got around. Then some asshole aristocrat accused me of cheating and shot me. Father frequented the hall and took pity on me, and here I am today."

"Were you cheating?"

"Of course, I was, sweetie," he says in an amused tone.

"Are these people all your friends?"

"Some," he says. "Mostly they're the ones who needed to see Father up and about again. They'll help to spread the news. It caused quite the stir when he said he was going to sleep for a century. They need to know he's back and not to be messed with."

"But he doesn't sleep."

"Deny us blood for long enough and we slip into something like a coma. You or I wouldn't have the strength to wake ourselves. But Father is old, with a singular sort of will, and I am sure you smelled absolutely delicious."

More of the guests are wandering outside to keep an eye on us. *So* weird. "Tonight is another show of strength?"

"Yes. Exactly. Vampires love a good turf war. They find it all very exciting, stealing each other's shit and slaughtering so-called friends. Gives them something to do to pass the time. We're not all like that, but enough of them are to be a problem. It's the issue with living forever; one gets jaded. Not even the board and their rules could stamp it out entirely. So it saves time if we show the idiots it's a bad idea to mess with our family. Even if there are only a few of us gathered here presently."

"But Lucas and Archie weren't friends."

"Not even a little. They never got along. But Archie kept up his attempts to reach Father over the last thirty years purely because he didn't want him waking up and claiming his territory. Guess he had a point. The runes never weakened, however, and I remained close at hand, so here we are." He leans against one of the pergola posts with his arms crossed over his chest. "Father flouted the rules by making you and then refusing to allow them to execute you. And whether he likes it or not, he's now the power to beat, in this neighborhood, at least. People need to see us strong and united."

"How were these guests able to get past the runes?"

"Because Lucas allowed it." Henry smiles. "He can have an open-door policy if he chooses. The runes behave according to his wishes. Especially now that he's awake."

"Are runes how the myth started about vampires needing to be invited into a home?"

"No. That one's true. But a human needs to live in the building. It must be someone's home," he says, tucking a strand of blond hair behind his ear. He has a number of piercings. "All these questions. Hasn't Father told you anything?"

"Only bits and pieces."

"Whatever created us ensured we had weaknesses," he says. "Running about in the daylight will turn you toasty. We can't enter a human's home without invitation, but any other building is up for grabs. Silver stings to touch. But a stake through the heart will ruin your entire night."

"What about crosses and garlic?"

"Bollocks. Complete nonsense. Once upon a time, a pope was being pressured to come up with a solution to us preying on his clergy. The next thing you know, we're supposedly all super religious with a dislike of seasonings. Idiot."

"Huh. Can Lucas sense where we are?" I ask. "I know he can do that tug thing where you feel him in the middle of your chest. You know, when he wants something. But can he actually tell where we are?"

"No. We can feel that tug, as you call it, from a distance. That's him telling us he wants us to phone home or something. And he can compel us if we're face to face. But it isn't supernatural GPS. He can't find us through the bond. Not still thinking of leaving, are you?" Henry tips his head. "I wasn't lying when I said you don't want to be on your own right now."

"No."

"Hm." He sighs. "It can be a hard and lonely life, this one. Centuries pass and we remain unaltered. Human lives are bright but fleeting. Give the family a chance to grow on you, sweetie. You never know; you might quite like some of us."

The way we're being stared at is annoying. And I've had enough.

Henry grins. "Look at you with the power moves."

"What?"

"You turned your back on them. It means you're not afraid of them attacking you. Very girl boss. Don't turn back around, you'll ruin it."

"I was just sick of them staring." I shake my head. "Does everything have to mean something?"

"Immortals tend to overthink things. Thanks to all of that time on our hands."

"Great."

"Father is something of a legend among our kind. It makes them curious. He hasn't made another vampire since me, and that was centuries ago," he says. "They're wondering what it means that he turned you. And they're wondering how strong his blood has made you. I got challenged all the time for the first decade or so. Tedious as fuck."

"You said he swore off making any more."

He nods. "Yes. But that's his story to tell. He wouldn't appreciate me sharing. What you really need to understand, Skye, is that we're his family. We're both his strength and his weakness. He was alone for a long time. It takes a lot for a creature like him to embrace the concept of sharing his long life with others."

"I highly doubt he cares about me one way or another," I say. "Saving me from those vampires last night was just a show of strength, like he said. And making me was an act of guilt or pity, as you inferred."

"Perhaps. Though, the blonde hair and green eyes wouldn't have hurt."

"That's the second time you've mentioned that. Why is it important?"

"You found an outfit you liked?" asks Lucas, appearing beside me, holding a full wine glass. If he heard me talking smack about him, it doesn't show.

He's been in a meeting in a room on the lower floor for hours. No idea who with. The black pants, button-down shirt, and shoes he has on all look expensive. It sucks how well he wears them. The man has pretty privilege and then some.

I do not want to be attracted to him. However, my gaze strays and then sticks to the strong line of his neck and the way the top three undone buttons reveal a glimpse of his chest, and this is not okay. Crushing on sociopaths is never a good idea. It's in bad taste on the part of my hormones to notice him in this way at all.

As for him being my sire, I *have* a father, and it is not him. Henry and Lucas can have whatever relationship they like. But we're a family in the loosest terms possible, as far as I'm concerned.

"Um. Yes," I say. "Thank you."

Henry smiles. "She cleans up well. Doesn't she, Father?"

Lucas nods and takes in my black designer velvet suit and heels. Henry convinced me not to wear a top beneath the jacket. But it's not like it doesn't button up to just below my bust. The bulk of me is covered, and no longer having to worry about gravity definitely has its perks. Four-inch heels are also easier to handle, given my vampire grace.

Henry took over doing my makeup after I accidentally broke the shower door and snapped a hairbrush. Controlling my strength is still hit or miss, apparently. My new brother has a variety of talents, including contouring. But it would be boring living forever without learning new things.

"Very nice," says Lucas, with a vague frown. Like he's not quite sure if me dressing up is allowed. But it's the word *beautiful* that appears in my head. Which is curious. His gaze lingers on my dark red lips. Not a color I would normally wear, but Henry was insistent. Guess he was right.

Lucas turns to face the guests gathered nearby and looks each and every one in the eye. They all break eye contact first. Then he turns to me and hands me the wine glass full of blood. "Drink this. It's one of your blood bags."

"The contents came from one of tonight's guests. Cage-free and consent-certified," says Henry with a smirk. "No humans were compelled in the production of tonight's sustenance."

Lucas ignores him. "You need to stay ahead of the hunger. Open your hand, and I'm going to place the glass into your grip carefully. Try not to break it. It was a gift from an empress."

"You always did admire Catherine," says Henry. "Remember that time outside of Druzhba when Benedict and I got you drunk by feeding on those inebriated aristocrats and we chased some bears?"

"Poor bears. Thank you." I accept the glass as delicately as possible and yes. Success. "If he calls you father, what am I supposed to call you, daddy?"

"I don't entirely hate the sound of that." A fleeting smile crosses his lips. He's even more handsome when he smiles. Devastatingly so. "We can talk about it later if you like."

Henry snorts.

"It was a joke," I say. "First names are fine. Who's Benedict?"

"Someone who is not here," answers Lucas, watching the crowd. And that's all he says, as per the usual. Keeping secrets doesn't make him half as alluring and mysterious as he seems to think it does. All right, so it probably does. But it is still a deeply annoying habit.

I take another sip of blood. "Okay. Next question. Do we get any other gifts when we change?"

"Like what?" asks Lucas.

"I don't know. Like reading minds, or starting fires with our thoughts, or stuff like that."

"Not that I've heard of," says Henry.

Lucas studies me. "It's very rare. Why are you asking, Skye?"

"No reason." I take another sip. "Just watched too many vampire movies, I guess."

His gaze narrows on me.

I stare back at him, transfixed. It's the same way I feel with the humans and their irresistible blood. As if I have a need only he can meet, which is absolutely not the case at all. The way my nipples have hardened to peaks beneath my jacket, however, is not helping.

"Have you fed recently?" asks Henry, interrupting the staring contest. Thank goodness. "You're looking a little hungry, Father."

"It's next on my list of things to do."

"Monica," Henry calls out to a woman in a slinky dress, curled up on the lap of another vampire. "Come here, please." Then he turns back to us and says, "We met in the VIP section at a Stage Dive concert last year. A charming girl, and a vegan, which gives the blood such an interesting taste."

Monica is gorgeous, with olive skin and shoulder-length, curly brown hair. She's naturally graceful. She doesn't even need vamp juice to make her so. And I am not the least bit jealous at all because that would just be weird.

Lucas's gaze fixes on her and his whole body goes statue still. Like he's about to pounce or something. Then a smile curves his lips, and he takes her hand and leads her farther back into the garden without a word.

I watch until they're out of sight, for some reason. It must be a newborn thing. Being clingy with the vampire who killed me and made me drink his blood, etcetera. Nothing else makes sense. Because I don't actually care about him walking away with someone else.

"Don't worry, he'll be back in a minute." Henry bumps his shoulders against mine with a smile. "Well, maybe not a minute. He hasn't gotten laid in over seventy years. It wouldn't surprise me if he's forgotten how to do it. Do you think I should go back there and give him some pointers? Remind him of what goes where? There are bound to be some anatomy books around here I could use."

I sip my blood and keep my mouth shut.

"No. You're probably right. Father doesn't have much of a sense of humor," says Henry. "Thank goodness you're here, little sister. Where would I be without you?"

"No idea."

"Me neither." He grins. "Fucking and feeding go exceptionally well together. You should try it sometime. Mind you, mortals can be so fragile. Are you any good at dancing?"

"Well—"

A shout comes from inside as a large figure strides through the French doors and out into the garden. It's the guard from last night with the shaved head and suit. The one who was guarding the steel door in the subbasement level of The Boulevard Hotel. Everyone gives him a wide berth, but they don't go anywhere. Heck no. They're all gathering outside, eyes alight with excitement at whatever's about to happen.

"Oh, shit," mumbles Henry.

"What?" I ask.

"Lucas," the man shouts. "We have business, you and I."

Lucas appears opposite him in a blur of motion. He wipes blood off his chin and says, "Hello, Berin."

"I didn't challenge you last night because I didn't want to disgrace the board. But I've resigned my position now. It's time for you to answer for his death."

"Archie doesn't deserve your loyalty."

"Perhaps not. But he made me. I was a member of his guard for almost a century."

"How did he get past the runes?" I whisper.

Henry leans closer. "Father considers him a friend. At least, he did."

"I understand," says Lucas, with sadness in his eyes. "It's a matter of honor. Are you ready?"

Berin nods.

It isn't as quick as when he killed Archie or Christos. They charge each other, hands grappling and pummeling. Lucas breaks loose and spins, slamming his elbow into the other male's nose. I wince at the sound of breaking bone. When blood spurts, a moan rises from the gathered guests, and they lean closer.

Berin bashes his fist into Lucas's cheek, making his head rock back. A flash of pain crosses his face, there and gone, and I lunge forward without thought.

Henry grabs me around the waist and anchors me against his hard body. "No, you don't, sweetie. You would only distract him. He wouldn't thank you for interfering."

"But—"

"Look closely," he says, lips brushing against my ears. "You can track his movements, can't you? You can see him?"

I nod. "Lucas isn't moving as fast as he can. He's letting him hit him."

"That's right," says Henry. "He's letting his friend get some hits in before he ends the fight. He's doing him a kindness."

"Didn't Berin know he couldn't win?"

"Without a doubt." Henry scoffs. "But some choose to find meaning in eternity by living by archaic codes or some such nonsense. Self-righteous wankers."

Lucas doesn't drag it out, however. Soon enough, he has the other vampire on his knees in a headlock. The smaller cuts and bruises on their faces are healing as we watch. Nice to know we have accelerated healing.

"Don't make me do this, Berin."

"My honor," is all the other male says in his strained voice.

Lucas's lips flatline. Then he punches his hand through the male's back and pulls out his heart. The body slumps in his hold before turning to ash. And that is that.

"Father didn't exactly have many friends to begin with," whispers Henry. "Now he has one less."

I say nothing.

Lucas straightens and turns our way. Ash covers his fine suit and blood drips from healing cuts on his cheek and lip. He allowed himself to be beaten black and blue. His forehead is furrowed, and shadows fill his gaze. Like all of the long years of his life are suddenly weighing heavily on his broad shoulders. The grief and loneliness in his expression is acute.

A polite round of applause starts among some of the guests and several of the humans raise their glasses in a toast to his victory. What idiots. Like this death was in any way a victory.

Lucas turns on them all with a snarl. "Get the fuck out of my house."

The whole pack flees like their asses are on fire. If Lucas wanted a show of strength, this has definitely achieved that end. But at what cost?

"Best thing to do when he gets this way is distract him. Otherwise, the gloominess goes on for weeks," whispers Henry.

"What?"

"Oh Father!"

I suddenly realize Henry has a pants situation. How embarrassing. I definitely wasn't pressing my butt against him on purpose. He was just holding me that damn tight. I wrestle out of his hold and the jerk grins.

"Distract him with what?" I ask. "Henry?"

Instead of answering me, he announces at the top of his voice, "You're never going to believe this. Awkward timing, I know. But her lust is kicking in and she smells fucking amazing."

## CHAPTER SIX

"Henry." I take another step back from him. There may or may not be things happening in my panties, but they're sure as hell nobody else's business. And the way Lucas is now staring at me is not good. "What the hell are you talking about?"

"The horniness is all part of the change," answers Henry. "It's totally normal and nothing to be ashamed of. I'm more than happy to help you out if you like, sister."

I hold up a hand. "Please stop talking. Just...no."

Meanwhile, Lucas has started growling low in his throat.

"Father." Henry laughs in delight. "Is this you actually being possessive, or are you just a little overstimulated from feeding and fighting, hmm?"

"Go away, Henry," says Lucas. "Now."

Monica stumbles out of the back garden with her hand to her neck. Her gaze is dazed, her color off. "Hey, what's happening? Was someone yelling?"

"Hello there." Henry smiles. "Let's get you a glass of juice, hmm?"

"With vodka," she says. "He took a lot."

"You really shouldn't drink on a depleted bloodstream." And he steers her off toward the house.

Lucas walks toward me in his ash-stained suit. The cuts on his mouth and cheek have closed now, though the spilled blood has yet to dry. He really did let Berin beat the shit out of him. "It's not only blood you want when you're newly turned."

"I'm fine. Thanks for the concern."

"Henry was right, it's nothing to be ashamed of."

"I am not ashamed."

"Your body undergoes all sorts of changes," he says in the same calm tone as he closes in on me. The bruising around his eye changes color from black and blue, to green and yellow, to back to normal. "An increase in lust is just another."

"I'm sorry you had to kill your friend." I press my hand against his hard chest, stopping him from getting any closer. "But I'm not a shiny new toy to distract you from your troubles."

"Of course not," he says. "You're different. You're mine."

"What?" I frown. "*No.*"

"I made you. I care for you. You're mine."

"You care for me? Bold of you, given you've threatened to kill me several times in the last twenty-four hours."

"And yet you're still here and unharmed."

"If a little undead." I shake my head. Being cast adrift in a world of night with him as my guide is a lot. "Lucas, this is not how I see our relationship progressing. A mentorship kind of situation is necessary. Maybe we can even stretch it into friendship in a century or two, when I've had a chance to calm down and process my trauma over you killing me. But nothing more. Not with you."

He leans in and sniffs me. Like an animal. "Henry was right. You do smell amazing. And the way you look..."

"Thanks. But still no."

"You're funny." He smiles. "I wasn't asking."

"What?"

Before I can say another word, he turns me. We're in the same position Henry and I were earlier. My back pressed to his front and his arms tight around me. "Look at the stars, Skye. I saw you watching them earlier. They're spectacular, aren't they?"

"Lucas," I say in a firm tone. "Let me go."

"You need to learn to trust me."

"I don't think the words you're saying mean what you think they do."

He pins my wrists behind my back with one hand, the other hand already undoing the buttons of my coat. "I can't remember much about my mortal life. But I can remember so clearly how on that first night, the whole sky seemed to come to life."

"Leave the buttons alone. You're getting blood and ash on my suit."

"I'll buy you another," he says. "I'll buy you whatever the fuck you want. Of course, there were no city lights to compete with back then. Still, it was awe inspiring. More than the strength and speed, it was being able to see the stars like that."

This isn't like when Henry held me. My awareness of him physically was next to nil. Don't get me wrong, he's an attractive boy. But that's exactly what he is, an extremely old fuckboy.

Lucas, on the other hand, feeds the lust higher. The way he holds me is both firm and gentle at the same time. His body is bigger and stronger, and his voice...there's something hypnotic about it. When I struggle and get nowhere, part of me almost doesn't mind. Proving once and for all that my hormones have terrible taste. Just the absolute worst. Giving in, however, is not an option. Not with him.

"I don't care if you haven't gotten laid in seventy years," I say, turning and tugging on my wrists to try and escape. "Get your pity sex elsewhere."

His laugh is low and rough. "No one talks to me like you. Even Henry respects my limits. But you just say whatever comes to mind, don't you?"

"Lucas..."

"Relax. We're not fucking. I don't think that would be a good idea," he says. "You strike me as the sort who takes intercourse too seriously."

"Wait a minute. You think I've never just hooked up? Really?"

"Hooked up?" he repeats. "What an interesting phrase. As I was saying, I have no interest in suffering through the infatuation of a newborn discovering vampire sex. This is purely a one-time thing. I'm just going to deal with your little problem and then I'll let you go."

"How about you don't do me any favors and let me deal with it on my own."

"Hm. No." He undoes the last button and pushes my coat open, baring my breasts in the black lace bralette. The hold on my wrists tightens as he sighs. "Skye, look at you. Fuck. You're so pretty."

"You thought I was homely."

He pauses. "I never said that."

And that's the truth. I heard the thought inside my head. But I am not in a mood to talk about it right now. "I don't want this, Lucas. Do you hear me?"

"Oh, you want it." He presses his nose against the side of my face and inhales the scent of me again. And the way he groans. "Your body is practically screaming for it."

"My body is an idiot and my brain knows better. And if we're not having sex, why are you undressing me?"

"Like I was saying, I've always enjoyed a view." His fingertip trails from my throat down, down, down. Between my breasts and over my stomach. Just when I think he's going to put his hand in my pants, he smooths his palm over the front of my suit pants. Which is absolutely a relief. Any other thought is an anomaly. "What Henry said reminded me," he says. "You wanted to talk about consent?"

"You're not funny."

"I have to agree with you. Humor has never been my talent. But I *have* been told I'm good with my hands." His hand curves over my crotch and presses firmly. And the pressure is wonderful. Like my favorite vibrator and showerhead working in tandem.

My insides squeeze tight, and oh wow. This is so wrong. He is still the asshole who killed me. I go up on my tiptoes, trying to escape him, but it's useless. He can probably feel how wet I am even through the material of my panties and pants.

The pad of his thumb finds my clitoris and applies the same delicious pressure. I can feel myself coming already. And I am never this fast and ready. It must be a vampire thing.

Heat shoots through me from top to toe. All of it centering on my sex. My nipples ache and every inch of skin feels oversensitive. Like the night air on the sides of my breasts and belly is enough to push me over. But it's his damn touch and his voice that does it.

"So beautiful," he whispers into my hair.

A sob catches in my throat and it's all too much. The moon and stars could disappear from the sky and I would neither notice nor care. My head falls back on his shoulder and my body shudders as the sensation goes on and on. Another vampire benefit, apparently. Orgasms that are out of this world. It's as if I've been born anew to pleasure and sin. And throughout it all, he holds me so tight it's like nothing bad can touch me. Nothing can ever hurt me again. With the exception of him, of course.

How embarrassing. It was so easy for him to decimate me. I didn't feel an ounce of shame before, but for some reason I am full of it now. I push out of his hold and this time he lets me go. Just as well. Then he just stands there in the dark, looking as handsome as sin, watching me with those immortal eyes.

I do my buttons back up with fumbling fingers. The horrible thing is, he's taken the edge off the lust. But I could so easily fall to my knees and beg for more. And I bet he knows it too.

"What?" I snap.

"Honestly?" He shrugs. "I was half expecting you to try and hit me."

I turn my back on him and walk toward the house. "Henry, I want to go out."


The nightclub is all polished concrete and metal. People pack the downstairs dance floor and bar area. It goes without saying that I've never been in a VIP section before. But Henry leads us straight past security and up the stairs to the mezzanine level, full of white leather lounges, low lighting, and glass tables. A supermodel, some A-list actors, and half a rock band are spotted in the first five minutes. Apparently, this is the place to be. At least there's small chance anyone I know would frequent here. As much as I dislike leaving my own life and plans behind, it's best if no one knows I didn't die in that fire. Though, part of me wonders if anyone would even recognize me now.

I changed my coat for a black V-neck tee and Lucas swapped out his suit for another, exactly the same. Lord knows how much they cost. The cut and style are immaculate. He could be the poster boy for fashionable undead capitalists everywhere. His dark hair is slicked back, and his gaze is constantly on the move, taking in everything. The Rolls-Royce Ghost that we found waiting in the garage, alongside a Bugatti Chiron, also pleased him immensely. This century seems to be a win for him.

Of course, the great thing about being a vampire in a nightclub is neither having to yell to be heard over the music, nor needing to line up to use the bathroom. Guess we just absorb the blood we drink. Very useful.

Nicole and I used to frequent a bespoke cocktail bar a few blocks away. A more simple and subdued setting. Less pulsating lights and blaring music. We would drink gimlets and talk about life and books and everything. I miss my best friend, and it's barely been a day. Staying away from the people I love is going to be hard. It is strange feeling lonely when you're surrounded by people. And I'm not the only one who has lost a friend recently. Not that I pity him exactly.

"You're staring at him again, sweetie," says Henry.

"I am very angry at him for multiple reasons. It's going to take me a while to process them all."

Henry shrugs. "You have to understand, he comes from a time when the head of the family had the last say in everything, and women, in particular, had fuck-all rights."

"That is no excuse."

"No," he allows. "But it does explain a few things."

"It explains nothing. He's perfectly intelligent enough to adapt and not behave like an asshat."

"Well, yes, but what would be the fun in that?"

I narrow my eyes on my new brother.

He just laughs. "Father's always been a broody bastard. Even when we were in Paris in the 1800s, drinking blood full of absinthe and opium, he was somber, at best. It's entertaining to watch him navigate you and the modern world. Turning you has honestly done him a world of good. Reinvigorated him to no end."

"That's just so wonderful to hear," I say drily.

"You don't really miss your mortal life, do you?"

"Yes. My life was boring, not bad. I have no idea what *this* is, apart from violent and complicated, and having way too much to do with him."

He nods. "Give it time. You're in mourning."

"What? For myself?" I ask with a smile.

And he nods again.

Lucas stands at the railing nearby, watching the mass of dancers writhe below. All of that seething humanity seems to fascinate him. He doesn't even blink as he takes it all in.

But enough about him. I will not let him ruin the second night of my bizarre new life. Being in a place like this with my enhanced senses is interesting. The play of lights dazzles my eyes, and I can feel the thump of the bass loud and clear through my breastbone. With my newfound stamina, I could dance all night. And who knows, I just might.

A bottle of Cristal champagne sits in a bucket of ice alongside some CÎROC vodka. It is all to lure in the humans and help us blend. However, it hardly seems required. They watch us with open fascination. Care of a preternatural je ne sais quoi or the undead glow up, I have no idea. But they hardly make hunting for sex or blood a chore. It is unprecedented. People are giving me come-hither glances. I ignore all of them because awkward. As someone who moved through life largely unnoticed, the change is extreme.

"I should be upset that you're Father's new favorite. Do you have any idea how boring it was while he was asleep?" Henry pouts. "Now he's awake again and it's all about you. You're very lucky I am so understanding."

"Sorry."

Henry crooks a finger at Monica, who is currently dancing and flirting over at the bar. "Time to teach you something. After all, knowledge is power, sweetie."

Monica sits between us with a grin and a glass of champagne and orange juice. Any earlier lack of energy or color has been remedied. With a finger to her chin, Henry smiles, stares deep into her eyes, and says, "Be a dear and cluck like a chicken, would you?"

"Henry," I scold. "Don't be a dick."

But the woman is already making clucking noises. She's even throwing in pecking motions for good measure.

"It's not hurting her. This sort of thing takes a lot of practice, but you can do it to any human unless they have a particularly strong will. Your turn," he says, nodding to me. "Now, you have to focus. Push your intent at them."

"Monica?" I angle my head to put myself in her line of sight. Not sure if screwing up my face and thinking hard enough to give myself a headache is necessary. But she does pause and stare back at me. "Go have a good night."

"What?"

"Really push," murmurs Henry. "Like I said...it's not easy. Most of us don't get this down for a decade or more. Push, Skye."

"I am trying," I say.

Her gaze shifts to Henry before returning to me. The woman's smile is definitely bemused. "What's going on?"

"Keep your eyes on me."

"Okay."

It's like I imagine a link between us. My thoughts in her mind. My will taking over her. Which is a beyond gross idea if you think about it. But here we are. I push and focus, and it's as if the world quiets around us. Something that might be down to my concentrating so hard. However, the temporary stillness feels a little like when I hear a word. I choose to take it as a positive sign. "Go have a good night, Monica."

"You want me to go?" she asks uncertainly.

"Do what you like. Have fun. Take care of yourself, okay?"

A hesitant smile fills her face, then she jumps up and heads back to the bar. This time stopping next to a curvaceous Black woman with piercings and a shaved head. Hand in hand, they soon leave together.

Henry rolls his eyes. "All of the things we can do. The complete control we can wield over their tiny, dull little lives. And you tell her to go be merry and stay hydrated."

"Do no harm, dude."

"Sister. Oh my God. We're apex predators. I am not sure if you actually had her, or she just liked the idea of taking the rest of the night off. Probably the latter."

"We can't tell if it's happening?"

"No. It's a subtle skill. You get to recognize the feel of doing it yourself when the connection is made. But apart from the blank stare on their faces, there's no way of telling if a human is being compelled by another," he explains. "Which is a definite downside to that little trick. Never mind. As Father has a habit of saying, practice makes perfect."

"Right."

He rises to his feet. "Back in a moment."

As soon as Henry is gone, an athletic-looking man in jeans and a fitted button-down shirt sidles on over. He's handsome, with tanned skin and a wide, white smile. In his mid-thirties at a guess.

"I don't have any good come-on lines," he says. "But can I join you anyway?"

I laugh. "Sure. Why not?"

"Come here often?" he asks with a comedic wince.

"Ooh. Now that's a classic. And the answer is no. This is my first time."

"I'm Aiden."

"Skye."

"Skye," he repeats with a flirty smile. "Good to meet you. How do you like the place?"

"It's great."

And this is all so bizarre, a man like this one making eyes at me. Having the vampire benefits feels like cheating. Though, it's not like I asked for them. Henry may have had a point. I need to loosen up and learn to have a little fun. It's either that, or stay home and read books for eternity. Which actually doesn't sound that bad, now that I come to think of it. But back to the here and now. I like having a pretty man smile at me.

"I own it." He nods to the nightclub at large. "We just opened a few months back."

"Really?"

He shuffles closer and leans in, and I catch the scent of his blood. Just that easy. The sound of it pumping through his heart. The sight of it so close to the surface beneath his warm skin. Guess the loud music and mess of scents in the place kept the need under control until now. But no longer.

"I, um..." I move farther away along the low lounge.

He frowns and makes to follow. "Are you okay?"

"Get any closer and she'll rip your throat out," says a low, dangerous voice. "Or if she doesn't, I will."

I reach for his hand, panicking ever so slightly. "Lucas."

Lucas pulls me to my feet and wraps his arms around me, crushing my breasts against his chest. "I told you, you need to stay ahead of it."

Aiden is already walking away. He's probably summoning security. What a mess.

"What's wrong?" asks Henry.

"She got hungry," says Lucas. "You were supposed to watch her."

"I was only gone for a moment."

"Can you walk out of here?" Lucas asks me.

"Yes."

To be so strong and so weak at the same time is infuriating and frightening. Now that I've tuned in to the blood, I don't know how to block it out. My hands are shaking, and my mouth is watering, and oh shit. I should never have asked Henry to take me out. What a stupid idea. If I kill someone, it will absolutely be my own damn fault.

Halfway down the stairs, Lucas stops and swings me up into his arms. Carrying me with an arm around my back and the other beneath my knees. "Put your arms around my neck, Skye."

I do as told, holding on tight. "Don't let me hurt anyone."

He jerks his chin in response.

The crowd surges around us as we skirt the edge of the dance floor. His hands dig into me, anchoring me against him. Henry gets in front of us and clears a path to the door. There is definite flashing of fang. Some of the startled expressions on the patrons' faces would be hilarious under any other situation.

The scents of smoke and sweat and alcohol fade as we reach the sidewalk outside. We wait for the new car to be bought around.

"I say we go home and start catching Father up on history and advancements in technology over the past almost a century. Start him off with some basic programming languages, and then round it all out with superhero movies. What do you think?" Henry gives me a gentle smile. But the word that appears inside my head is *disappointed*.

"I'm sorry I ruined your night out," I say.

"It's fine." He frowns. "You didn't."

"Put me down, please. I think I'm okay now." A part of me feels safe in Lucas's arms. And that part of me needs to learn better. As he said, he doesn't need any clingy newborns cramping his style.

Lucas looks me over before doing as asked. Guess I don't seem quite so on the edge of attacking anyone. I stand there with my arms wrapped tight around myself, thinking calm thoughts.

The traffic has thinned out at this time of night. There's still a line of people waiting to get into the club. A silver Escalade cruises toward us, a back window lowering to let in the night air. The person behind the wheel is wearing sunglasses and a sneer.

And the word that fills my head like a shout is *gun*.

"Get down!" I scream, and throw myself at the two males. It's a bad attempt at a tackle. They're both more than strong enough to stay standing. But working at superspeed, Lucas looks around and sees the vehicle.

Understanding fills his face, and he moves to cover Henry and me. We're on the ground before the first bullet flies. The report of the weapon is ear-shatteringly loud. So, too, are the screams of the humans around us.

# CHAPTER SEVEN

"Wooden bullets." Lucas examines the ammunition in his hand. "Amazing."

"Welcome to the twenty-first century, Father," says Henry. "Two attempts on your life in one night. That's when you know you've really made it. We'll have Dracula knocking on the door challenging you to a dance-off next."

We're back at the house in the basement living room. Dawn is still several hours away, but going underground seemed safest. The runes won't stop a sniper from shooting us through one of the upstairs windows. Henry said that was unlikely, however, because wooden bullets aren't as heavy or strong as metal ones. I still wonder if bulletproof glass for the house will be next on the shopping list. The only good news tonight is that no one else was hurt outside the nightclub.

We got out of there as fast as possible. Then Lucas made a call to Helena, and Henry called someone else, and things were set in motion. Our asses are apparently covered in case of any security cameras, and where the local authorities are concerned. Vampire politics seem to be a lot like organized crime. Violence, money, and secrets. This is assuming what film and TV taught me about them is true.

I spent the ride home downing a blood bag. Handy that the Rolls-Royce had a stocked fridge. The Thorn Group really does think of everything.

Lucas puts a Louis Armstrong record on while I hug an embroidered silk cushion to my chest. "Are we assuming this is about Archie?"

"Seems likely," he says. "Skye, how did you know?"

My gaze jumps to his face.

"The gun wasn't in sight yet when you reacted," he continues. "You were asking earlier about the possibility of extra gifts being bestowed when you're turned. Is there something you want to tell me?"

I choose my words with care. "I wasn't sure if it meant anything at first. It was mostly just a random word appearing in my head now and then. Like it was giving me a hint of what someone was thinking."

He nods.

"Then I looked at the driver of the Escalade and he was staring at us, and I heard the word *gun* inside my mind," I say. "Given they'd only just rolled down the back window, I jumped to the conclusion that it was a drive-by shooting and we were the targets and reacted accordingly."

"You only hear one word?"

"Yes."

Henry frowns. "What if the word is like *the* or *and*?"

"That would be incredibly unhelpful," I say. "But apparently that's not how it works. When we were outside the club, I heard the word *disappointed* from you. It seems to be a random mix of things that people near me are feeling. And it's not constant, just now and then."

"Such as when I thought you were homely," says Lucas.

The way I hesitate says more about my feelings than I like. "Yes."

"Father," gasps Henry. "How rude. And blatantly incorrect, I might add. She's gorgeous."

"I wonder if, with practice, you could train yourself to tune into a mind." Lucas taps out a beat on the arm of the chair. "I have only met a couple of other vampires with gifts such as this. One who could move things with his mind, and another who could read objects. Get a feel for where they had been and suchlike. These vampires were treasured and well-protected members of their families. But both of their gifts developed over time."

"If word got out, people would definitely want her," says Henry, his gaze narrowed on me.

Lucas also stares as if he's reassessing me. Like he's surprised to find I have sudden hidden value. It is honestly a bit much after everything.

I rise from the sofa. "I'm going to have a bath."

Covered in grit from the sidewalk and hints of ash from earlier, I could do with a wash. It doesn't take long for the old claw-foot tub to fill. I dump my designer wear on the floor and climb in. The water is deliciously hot and the room full of steam.

No idea why or when I start crying. Again. The last two nights have been intense. I want to talk to my best friend and get her take on all of this. I want to hear my mom's voice. And I really want to walk in the sunlight one last time and feel the warmth on my face. Woe is me.

The door cracks open and Lucas steps inside, closing it behind him. "I don't like the taste of your tears."

"You can taste my tears?" I ask with a sniffle. I press my knees to my chest and cross my arms to cover my breasts. "That's so bizarre. And I'd really appreciate it if you could find the key for that door so I can lock it when I want privacy."

"I could still just break it if I wanted to get in."

"Given how upset you get when I break something around here, I'm guessing you won't," I say.

"Your sadness fills the air."

"Go away, please."

"You've seen me naked," he says. "I'm not allowed to see you?"

"I didn't look at you. And no, not without an invitation."

"Consent again. It's not like I can see anything the way you're sitting." He kneels by the tub and rests his arms on the side and makes himself right at home. Okay, it *is* his home, but still.

"Why did you come in here, Lucas? What do you want?"

"I don't know." His forehead furrows as if he's genuinely mystified. "I just couldn't sit out there doing nothing while you cried."

"Since when do you care?"

"Again. I don't know. It's not like me." He thinks it over. "It would seem I've undergone some changes during my sleep."

"What was it like?"

"Painful for a while. The hunger for the first few months was fierce, but I was determined to wait it out. Then my body started to weaken, and my mind began to drift, going over old memories and such. It was similar to what I remember dreaming to be."

"Why did you do that to yourself?" I ask. "Just because you were bored?"

His smile is small. "No. I was...upset about something. Turning my back on this world for a while seemed safest."

I nod. Not that I understand a damn word.

"Now and then, one of the old ones loses their grasp on reason. They turn savage, slaughtering their families and anyone else nearby. Causing chaos until they can be stopped."

"You were worried that would happen to you?"

He shrugs. "My anger was very great."

"And now?"

The side of his mouth kicks up just a little. "Much better, thank you for asking."

While I am not ashamed of my body, hanging out with random, uninvited dudes while naked is a new thing. "Okay. I've stopped crying. You can go now."

"You don't need my assistance again with..." He just stares at me, waiting.

"Believe it or not, Lucas, I know how to masturbate just fine. And I thought you said that was a one-time thing. Something about a newborn's infatuation being yucky and inconvenient?"

He rises to his feet, all grace and strength. The expression on his face, however, is pure fuckery. "What did you call it, pity sex?"

"Get out."

"Skye," he says, waiting until he has my attention. Then, he says, "You were never homely. I was just being an asshole."

"I know."

At this, he nods his head. "Enjoy your bath."

I wake up the next evening with Lucas lying on the bed beside me again. Only the pants remain of his sleek suit. All of the dips and planes of his chest are on show. His bulging biceps, in particular, call to me. But then, the whole of him is like a work of art. Guess the unnatural horniness is still a thing. Because I refuse to be attracted to the monster under normal conditions. I have to be smarter than that. Surely.

This evening, he's busy with a digital notepad instead of a book. When I crashed, he and Henry had *Barbarella* playing on a laptop, while occasionally reading aloud from *The Feminine Mystique*, and also discussing the civil rights movement, the Vietnam War, and the moon landing. They seemed to have settled in for the day to discuss and debate at length each era Lucas had missed.

Having not been alive during the 1960s and with no hope of keeping up, I went to bed in my new, black silk pajamas. A definite step up from my usual panties and an old tee. And once again I was out as soon as my head hit the pillow. The newborn vampire need for sleep is no joke.

"Would you say you're Team Jacob or Team Edward?" Lucas asks contemplatively. "Because in all honesty, I'm having trouble deciding."

"Are werewolves real?"

"Yes. Though, they're generally not found around here because they don't like cities. Werewolves need space to run."

"Wow. Next question. Are you at all familiar with the concept of privacy?"

His brows draw together. "It's my bedroom."

"We need more beds. What's even in the other rooms down here? That hall goes halfway into the Hollywood Hills, but all the doors are locked."

"Things I've collected over the years."

"You're a hoarder," I say. "You know that, right?"

"Speaking of which...there's something for you on the bedside table."

I roll over—and holy shit. There are three familiar, slim, hardcover books waiting, bound in red with gold lettering. "Is that the first edition of *Pride and Prejudice* that was upstairs?"

"Henry noticed you admiring it," he says. "He said you were sad that you lost all of your belongings in the fire."

I don't know what to say.

Lucas suddenly looks up, tosses the notepad onto the bed, and blurs out of the room. Without a word. Like he's an animal that's caught a scent.

The speed at which I follow him is about half of his, at a guess. But my reactions work well, I don't crash into anything. I'm taking it as a win. Then Lucas, Henry, and I are on the front porch, staring at a stranger waiting patiently in the arched gateway of the stone fence. He's handsome, with dark skin and short hair.

"Woodsman."

"Father's nickname from way back," whispers Henry. "Not really a compliment. Long story."

Lucas gives me a cranky look. "You should have stayed downstairs."

I shrug.

"Captain," says Henry, with a smile. "Are you finally ready to take me up on my offer of a proper catch-up? We haven't hung out together in an age!"

"Not since 1863 after the Siege of Vicksburg." The stranger nods at Henry. "I learned my lesson about spending time with you when the humans tried to burn down the church I was sleeping in."

"How was I to know they'd be so touchy about us being undead and all?" Henry smiles. "It wasn't like we weren't helping them win. A bit of gratitude wouldn't have gone astray. But you wouldn't believe how good I made that uniform look, Skye. The blue really brought out my eyes."

The stranger shakes his head. "I never did understand why you turned him, Woodsman."

"It was largely due to my entertainment value," says Henry. "Someone had to be the court jester."

"We both know that's not the role you play in your family." The stranger raises a brow in question. "Are you going to invite me in?"

"Does Rose know you're here?" asks Lucas.

"She does."

Lucas frowns, pauses, and then nods. "Come in, Samuel."

"Let's give them a moment, shall we?" Henry slips an arm around my waist and ushers me back through the house. Pausing at the fridge to grab a couple of blood bags for me, of course. Then we head for the lounge room belowground.

"A long time ago, Father was a spy and enforcer for one of the oldies. The one who turned him, actually. Father liked to rely on word of mouth to do his job for him. He's always been a big believer in work smarter instead of harder. Every morning, when vampire children were tucked into bed, they were warned if they didn't behave, the Woodsman would get them."

"There are vampire children?"

"Fuck no. Who wants an immortal toddler or tween? Can you imagine anything worse?" Henry pushes his blond hair out of his face. "During that period, Father carried around this terrifying, big bloody axe. He's still got it around here somewhere. Basically, his job was to punish the naughty. He lopped off more than a few undead heads and limbs, let me tell you."

"That's why they're still so afraid of him?"

"Sweetie, in the forty-eight hours you've been a vampire, you've already seen him rip out hearts and tear off heads. I'd say their fear is warranted, wouldn't you?"

"Are you allowed to tell me this?" I ask. "Yesterday you wouldn't even say how old he was."

He takes a sip of my blood bag and pulls a face. "Ugh. I honestly don't know how you can drink that."

"Focus, Henry."

"I don't really think he'd mind me telling you just that much."

"I mind," says a voice from the direction of the front doorway.

"Oops." Henry winces. "Please don't chop off my head, Father. I'll be a good boy, I promise."

"Shut up and go check the area for any unwelcome visitors." Lucas enters the underground lounge with Samuel. "Skye, stay out of sight until he's given you the okay."

Henry takes off without another word. By the time I've finished my second blood bag, he's back, and it's officially safe to use the aboveground floors.

One thing about being a vampire, temperatures are no longer a problem. A bitterly cold wind is blowing. Not that it bothers me, particularly. But I find a black sweater and matching jeans in my armoire, along with a pair of designer boots. It is about as plain as my wardrobe goes. Being a member of this family means dressing the part, apparently. My hair is tied back in a ponytail, and I'm done. No need for me to be hanging out with strangers in my pajamas.

They're seated in the living room when I come downstairs. Lucas is wearing a black button-down shirt and shoes. Guess you don't entertain guests half naked. He signals me to join him on the chaise lounge.

I do as asked, but keep a good half foot of space between us. At least I'm being included in whatever this is. Henry, meanwhile, is picking out a tune on the piano, while Samuel has settled into a chair in the corner.

Outside, the night is quiet. Give or take the various insects and other animals. The neighbor to the left watches a movie, while the ones on the right eat an early dinner. Then there's the distant hum of traffic rising up from the Sunset Strip. But I'm getting better at blocking it all out. At only focusing on the information I need here and now.

"When did you leave London?" asks Lucas.

Samuel sets his ankle on the opposite knee and makes a show of getting comfortable. "A little over thirty years ago."

"Makes sense she'd want you with her during the cull. Someone she could trust to watch her back."

"We'd spent enough time apart."

Henry looks up from the keys. "Rose and Samuel have been married for centuries, Skye. It's quite the epic romance. They were wed in Morocco in 1762. Now *that* was a party."

"You'll have to forgive us." Samuel gives me a charming smile. "Vampires are such notorious gossips that we assume everyone already knows our business."

"Father balances out that fact by telling her nothing," says Henry.

Lucas frowns. "I'm not that bad."

"Eh," I say, because feedback is important.

"Samuel and Rose are mates. They always go back to each other in the end," finishes Henry.

"You mean like soul mates?" I ask.

Lucas shakes his head. "There's no proof those exist."

"Says the supernatural creature." Henry grins. "Call me a romantic fool, but I met this fascinating couple in Berlin a while back. It was when the wall came down. They'd been together even longer than Samuel and Rose. They met back when Genghis Khan invaded India and had rarely left each other's sides since. Can you imagine?"

Lucas's brows draw down. "Spending forever stuck with someone? No, thank you."

"I thought it was lovely." Henry pouts. "Not that I'm signing up for it or anything. What do you think, Skye? You're on my side, aren't you?"

"My longest relationship barely lasted a year." I smile. "What would I know?"

Lucas clears his throat. "Here's something you should be aware of, Skye. In Rose's family, Samuel plays the part of spymaster."

"I am, of course, unable to confirm if that is true or not." Samuel looks me over in silence for a moment. "Your Skye here is the first newborn made in the city in almost thirty years. It's been a long time since there's been any new blood in L.A. Guard her well. Some will be jealous that you got away with flouting the rules. Some will simply target her in an attempt to make you look weak."

"What really happened?" asks Lucas. "How did L.A. descend into rules and boards?"

Samuel's tongue plays behind his cheek. "The largest family in Russia was dissatisfied with their hunting grounds. They decided they needed more and turned their eyes to our fair city. Lev, the heir, was in charge of the operation. He had the money to buy a large following among the greedy and stupid. Then bolstered those numbers with newborns, and lots of them. All of those creatures out on the streets every night, causing bedlam and killing indiscriminately. Within no time at all, L.A. was in turmoil. The families had no choice but to send out their guards night after night to deal with the troublemakers."

"And that's when Lev tried to take them out?" asks Lucas.

"Yes." Samuel stares out at nothing. "He succeeded in destroying several of the midsize families. There were also attempted hits on Archie, Javier, and Rose. The board was hastily convened, and they didn't trust each other. It seemed unlikely they'd agree on anything. But the cull went ahead simply because they were so desperate for a solution. Lev, unfortunately, managed to escape the city and avoid being caught."

"I was this close to waking you, Father," says Henry, holding two fingers half an inch apart. "It was a shitshow."

Lucas frowns. "L.A. is a long way from Russia."

"The old ones love a land grab. You know that. And a juicy big war always staves off the boredom for a while."

"Why hold on to all of these rules and regulations for thirty years?" asks Lucas.

"You have to understand, what happened here in the nineties wasn't unique," says Samuel. "The vampire population had gotten out of hand everywhere. There were more of us than could safely share this world and its hunting grounds. To compound the problem, we'd gotten soft. The age of science made it easier to survive for a time. Humans became more rational thinkers, and no longer listened to the old stories. Many turned their backs on religion and those who would have warned them of things that go bump in the night. But there were also fewer of them for a while. A hundred-million lives were lost in the human wars of the last century. It's just as well; they fuck like rabbits and multiply quickly."

Henry plays a couple of bars of some piece at an up-tempo speed. His take on classical porn music, perhaps.

"But more importantly, technology changed. Governance changed. People don't tend to go missing anymore without any follow-up from the authorities. There are fingerprint and DNA databases."

"Henry explained to me about how far science has come," says Lucas. "It doesn't surprise me humans carry their individuality even into their blood. Any vampire could have told you as much."

"And it's not just DNA," Samuel continues. "Cameras are everywhere, and the methods of tracking us plentiful. Our race can't afford to have fools or careless newborns running around exposing us all to risk. The world is much more dangerous for vampires than it used to be," says Samuel. "We weren't the only ones to decide on population measures. Many families forbade the making of newborns and formed packs to destroy any creatures who strayed into their territories. Wars over hunting grounds broke out everywhere. Most families were diminished. Some were even wiped out entirely."

"These are dangerous times. A fool sat on a beach in Ibiza last year, waiting for the sun to come up. Broadcast it live on social media for all the world to see. It was written off as a stunt to promote a new horror movie. Lucky our bodies turn to ash and leave no evidence." Henry starts playing a piece by Chopin. "The nineties were a purge for our kind. There are guesses that our population dropped by almost seventy percent."

"Is that still happening?" asks Lucas.

"No. At least, not to the same degree," says Henry. "By the time the new century came around, our numbers were sufficiently lowered enough for everyone to relax. But from the reports I've received, the world out there still isn't as cushy as it once was, Father."

"We should have talked about this earlier," chides Lucas.

Henry sags on the piano seat. "I only just got you back. Forgive me if I wanted a few nights of fun before detailing the many ways in which the world went to shit while you were sleeping."

Lucas rests an arm on the back of the chaise and toys with the end of my ponytail. Picking up a lock of hair and winding it around his finger. This is odd behavior, to say the least. We're not touchy-feely friends. We're not even friends. Though, this seems like a serious conversation that is best not interrupted. I, therefore, give him the side-eye, but keep my mouth shut. My boot, however, shifts nervously against the Persian rug at my feet. Tonight, my body wants to move; sitting still sucks. I'm like a restless child.

"Why are you here, Samuel?" asks Lucas. "What do you want?"

"You have to take Archie's seat," he answers. "Anything else will make the board look weak and leave them open to challenge. You would be forcing them to move against you. As you can imagine, the laws have been unpopular. The board has already publicly committed to a lessening of them, along with reducing the presence of board members' guards on the streets. But Lev has been sighted in Seattle. We know his family didn't take well to his failure here. And the mess that is now your territory would appeal to anyone looking for a place to start some trouble."

"The house on Lake Como is lovely this time of year," says Henry. "Or the penthouse in Copenhagen. Fuck it. Even the draughty old castle in Scotland would be tolerable given the circumstances. Just in case anyone was wondering what I was thinking."

"The fact is, you weren't here to help sort shit out when we could have done with assistance, Lucas," says Samuel, in a brusque tone. "If you're going to stay in this town, you need to step up. We don't want another cull. But if Lev, once again, starts causing chaos, we may not have a choice."

"What's happening with Archie's family, now that he's gone?" asks Lucas, changing the subject.

"Some have gone into hiding. Some are being absorbed into other families," reports Samuel. "But even with his group diminished, one of Archie's guards, Joshua, is making a move. There are rumors that he was the family assassin, but we're having trouble confirming that. I find it unlikely, since my sources have confirmed that it was he who ordered the hit on you last night outside that club."

"Why not do it himself, if he's really the assassin?" asks Lucas.

"That's my thought."

"Wait. Someone named Josh tried to kill us?" asks Henry archly. "Are you serious?"

Samuel shrugs.

"Oh, his head is fucking mine. Like hell I'll have a *Josh* paying people to take shots at us."

Lucas holds up a hand for silence. The one that isn't busy playing with my hair. He pauses for a moment before saying, "I don't remember anyone of that name being particularly close to Archie. Was he the designated heir? Did he inherit the family money?"

"No. That's the interesting part." Samuel's smile is slow and kind of evil. "Archie kept his purse strings tight and his wealth well hidden. In the event of his unfortunate demise, it was all to go to his favorite. But you'd already dealt with Christos. It's going to take Josh a while to track down exactly what Archie did with it all.

"And in the meantime, Josh has no visible means of his own. He's only just over a century old, and not exactly good with finances, according to reports. He also made overtures to a disgruntled member of Javier's guard. One who's been vocal about his dislike of the board. Joshua offered him serious money for his sire's head."

"How do we know this?"

"Javier employs a hacker."

"That's someone who can break into computer systems," explains Henry. "Intercept electronic mail and messages and so on."

"Is someone funding Josh?" asks Lucas. "And if so, who?"

"That's the question," says Samuel. "But he's gone to ground and I can't find him. Wasn't even able to locate the marksman they used in last night's attempt. I will say it's a level of organization and secrecy I wasn't expecting. Until we figure out if someone powerful is backing him, we have no idea if the attempts on your family will continue, or how serious they'll be."

Henry sighs and plays some low, jarring notes. "You're going to have to send for them, Father."

"I already have." Lucas's face is a perfect blank. "All right, Samuel. Please tell your board that I accept the seat."

# ☾ CHAPTER EIGHT

The three of us escort Samuel out to a waiting limousine. Then Henry nods to Lucas and takes off into the night. Guess he's stalking the neighborhood again for enemies. I actually have enemies. Sort of. How bizarre. Not a problem I thought I would ever have, but here we are. It's good to be out in the night air. There are so many scents, sights, and sounds. A nervous sort of energy is running rampant through me. At least the horniness and hunger have calmed down for now. Or have they?

"Who have you sent for?" I ask, the moment we're alone.

Lucas's high forehead is full of furrows. It is a furrow farm. He still remains handsome as sin, however. It's not just the sharp angles of his face. There's something soulful and somber about his eyes. As if he's gazed into the abyss once too often over the course of his long life. "You'll see soon enough."

The way I want to slap him in frustration. But I don't, so bonus points for me. "Why did you change your mind about accepting the seat?"

"Did you know I've been in this town since 1862?"

"No."

"I've stayed in places longer. But when I built this house, it was because I wanted to put down roots. I like the city of angels, and I have no intention of leaving," he says, staring off down the dark and empty street. "Which means we need to start dealing with the problems here. Let's get back inside. You heard what Samuel said, you need to stay out of view until we have more information."

"What? No," I whine. "I'm sick of sitting around."

"I noticed."

"You have no room to talk. You were playing with my hair for half of that meeting."

Hands in his pants pockets, he wanders back into the house. "I was trying to soothe you. All of your foot tapping and fidgeting was distracting."

"I'm not an animal you can soothe by petting."

"Whatever you say." He heads back down the stairs and into the basement. "You did well moving quickly through the house when Samuel arrived. I half expected to find an imprint of your pretty face in my kitchen wall."

"I didn't hit anything, thank you very much."

"Then how about a game of chase?"

I pause. "What?"

"Go," he says with a tip of his chin. "Stick to the below-ground areas."

"But I can't outrun you."

"You're wasting time. Go."

"Shit," I mumble, and take off. Moving this way is a hell of a rush. Like my body flows through the house too fast to be seen. The world passes by in a flash, but my reflexes work just as quickly. I swerve to avoid furniture and walls and other immoveable objects.

I've never been a particularly sporty person. It's been decades since I felt the thrill of moving at genuine speed. The sense of power and sheer fun of it.

Soon I'm standing in the living room of the underground lair, and Lucas is right behind me. Dammit. The living room is spacious, but still. Whichever way I turn, he's already there, blocking me. And judging by the fang-filled smile on his face, he is enjoying this a lot. But hell, so am I.

He corners me against a wall, arms on either side of me, caging me in. "Skye, you're not even trying."

"I am, too."

"You're just going to give up and not even fight when I catch you?" he asks. "That's making it a little too easy for me. We're vampires, being hunted is par for the course. You need this practice. Try harder. Come on."

I duck beneath his arm and run. And he lets me go. Of course, he does. There's no way I could escape him otherwise, even with my amped-up abilities.

Lucas is old and strong and wily as heck. The next time he catches me, it's with my chest pressed against one of the locked doors in the hallway. Because where the hell else was I supposed to run? As much as I might have liked, the door hasn't mysteriously been unlocked, providing me with a handy escape. Nope.

"Let's chat," he says, pushing me against the door by pressing himself hard against my back. More than enough to remind me I am going nowhere without his permission. Also more than enough to remind me that he does, indeed, have a dick. "What I was wondering is, do you still hate me? Because I don't think you do."

"Still after the pity sex, huh?"

"You can talk." His low laughter does things to me. Things that shouldn't be allowed. "Skye, the scent of your sweet cunt...if I didn't know better, I'd think your fingers aren't quite up to the task of keeping you satiated after all. Now answer the question."

"Keep your mind out of my pants."

"Answer the question," he growls.

"Do I hate you? I don't know. You did kill me."

"Well, yes, but I brought you back to life. That's got to count for something."

"Wait. What are you doing? Are you sniffing me?"

First his nose and lips press lightly against the back of my neck. The way I'm breathing so fast when I don't need to be breathing at all is kind of awkward. Then the tip of a sharp fang is dragged over my bare skin, making me shiver.

"Lucas," I gasp. "That tickles."

"It tickles?" he says, sounding mildly outraged. But he steps back and slaps me hard on the ass with a grin on his face. "That's it. Next time I catch you, I'm biting you. Go."

"No. No biting."

"I'm a fucking vampire. Biting is what I do. Now run."

The hallway goes back into the hill, but all of the damn doors are locked. One of these nights I'm going to find out what he's hiding.

His fingertips slide over my arm as I slip past him and head back toward the living room. How he toys with me. In the living room, I upset an expensive-looking vase, but he's there, righting it before it can topple. Thank goodness. Through the basement and toward the stairs I go. Before I can escape up into the rest of the house, however, he's there blocking the way. My hair flies in my face with the sudden stop, and I teeter on my toes.

"I said to stay underground," he says in a stern voice. "Turn your ass around."

I do as told and race past the furniture and wooden chests and wine racks. Not breaking a thing. Yay me. His teeth snap a warning near my ear as I circle the living room. Then his arms are grabbing me around the middle, and the jerk tackles me onto a Persian rug. But it's a catch-and-release type situation, apparently. Because when I push up, he lets me keep going. Down the hallway and into his bedroom, where I try to shove the door shut in his face. Only he has a good grip and is pushing back, making my booted feet slide across the floor.

"You are not biting me!"

"So make me a counteroffer," he says. "What do you think you have that I want?"

"Nothing."

He laughs and the door flies open with a final push of his strength. I give up and head farther into the room. And putting the bed between us seems like a sensible idea.

He has, however, apparently decided we're done playing. Moving faster than I can track, he grabs me and throws me onto the mattress so hard, I bounce. But he's there to keep me put a moment later.

"Like I was saying." He grabs my wrists to anchor me. The way he makes himself at home in the cradle of my thighs feels far too good. Then he repeats, "What do you think you have that I want?"

"Absolutely nothing."

He smirks. "Now you know that's not true."

It is not absolutely thrilling having him all over me. My newborn horniness just roared back to life for some *other* reason. "Um. Let me think. I could give you texting lessons."

"Henry already showed me that during the day when you were asleep."

"How about social media? I could show you—"

"Pass."

"I don't know," I say. "Have you discovered computer games yet? I just know you'll be a Stardew Valley fan."

"Not interested," he says. "I think I'll take your mouth, instead."

"My what?" I ask in a haughty tone. "I'm not giving you oral."

He barks out a laugh. "Not what I meant."

"Oh."

"As if I would let your teeth anywhere near my dick without being first assured of your affections."

I laugh.

Then, without further ado, he kisses me.

I am too startled to react at first. But he doesn't hesitate. His mouth covers mine and his tongue slips inside, and huh. He really knows how to kiss. He traces my teeth and tongue, being gentle and demanding in turns. In no time at all, he seduces a reaction out of me, feeding me kisses deep and wet. The man goes straight to my head. No one has ever put this sort of single-minded determination into reducing me to a pile of mush. His body weighing me down and the firm grip he has on my wrists are my undoing.

It is heavenly having him this close. I can admit as much in the privacy of my own head. He kisses me deep and strong and true. Like nothing else matters. Like he's been saving this up for nights. Which makes no sense. He's rich and hot and immortal and could have anyone. While my standout attribute is my inability to keep my mouth shut and stop giving him shit.

And none of this explains why my legs are wrapped around his hips, holding him to me.

"I don't remember my training sessions with Father being quite so handsy," says Henry over by the door.

Lucas groans and raises his head. The way his nostrils flare at the intruders is pure pissed-off animal. It's kind of thrilling.

"We shouldn't judge," says another male with a curious accent. Nordic, at a guess. He'd make a great Thor. All tall and built with long blond hair and tattoos. "Maybe he's starting by teaching her wrestling. On a bed. With his tongue."

"Where the fuck have you been, Benedict?" asks Lucas.

"Here and there."

"You were supposed to be watching my back."

"I had other duties to attend to."

"What about me?" cries Henry. "I have valiantly watched over you for seventy fucking years. Where is the thanks!"

"I'm sure you did the best you could," says the large stranger. "Even though you somehow weren't there when Father woke. I am sure whatever you were doing was very important. There, there, little brother."

"You're the worst, Benedict. The absolute fucking worst."

Benedict gives us a nod. "Feel free to return to your training. We did not mean to interrupt."

"Of course, you realize he's not really going to train her. Not anytime soon, at any rate," says Henry.

"Why not?"

"He likes her soft. It's part of what makes her an anomaly in his world." Henry leans against the doorframe. "For example, she sleeps in his bed. Has done that ever since he turned her."

"You're kidding me?"

Lucas grunts but says nothing. And he stays put on top of me. Awkward as heck.

"When Father turned me, he threw me into his dungeon for weeks, leaving jugs of blood at the door once a night," says Henry. "Wouldn't let me out until I promised not to bite the staff or break any of his precious furniture."

"He chained me to a tree," says Benedict.

Henry's brows reach for the sky. "He chained you to a tree? Are you serious? How have I never heard about this?"

"You talk so much, I hardly ever get a word in." Benedict shrugs. "It was this big old oak. A very nice tree, but still...I had to burrow in the ground each day to stay out of the sun."

"You chained him to a tree?" I ask in amazement.

"It's a long story." Lucas finally climbs off me and offers his hand. "He kept trying to kill me."

Benedict nods. "I did, that's true. Our king tasked me with cutting off the evil creature's head. But Lucas liked how I fought and turned me."

"The Middle Ages were rough. I thought a Viking berserker might come in handy."

I blink. "Huh."

"What did you do for food when you were chained to this tree?" asks Henry.

"Before dawn each day, he would stand at a distance and throw rabbits at me," says Benedict in the same stoic tone.

Henry cocks his head. "What? Live ones?"

"No," says Lucas. "That would be cruel. I'd already wrung their necks."

"Let me just say again how sorry I am that we interrupted your training session," says the big dude with his bass voice. "Would you like us to go away until you're finished?"

"Shut up, Benedict," says Lucas. "It's good to see you."

"You, too, old man."

This vampire must be almost seven-foot tall. He is huge.

"And this must be my new sister Skye, whom I have heard so much about."

The word that enters my head when Benedict turns my way is *curious*. But it's surrounded in a warm glow of a feeling. Like he's happy to be here. Guess Lucas was right about my gift and its ability to grow. Seeing the feeling associated with the word could be very helpful.

"Hello," I say. "I see vampires come in size extra-large. How did Archie not steal you for his guard?"

Benedict snorts. "He tried. Many times. I understand he's no longer with us?"

"Father tore his head off." Henry puts a Robert Johnson record on the player. "You know what he's like when he's in a mood."

"He challenged me," says Lucas. "Sort of. Let's talk in the living room."

Benedict wanders back down the hallway, getting comfortable on a fancy-looking French chair. Henry flings himself into an armchair while Lucas takes a seat on the couch. Choosing to sit beside me for the second time tonight—which is weird.

"I'm not going to misbehave." I nod to the big old wingback sitting empty. "You can go sit on your throne."

Henry laughs. "Father's favorite chair does look like a throne, doesn't it?"

"I'm fine where I am," says Lucas, and nods to Benedict.

"Leilah will enter the city at sundown," reports Benedict. "She and her people will immediately move to infiltrate The Boulevard Hotel. She anticipates having it under family control by dawn."

"We'll be there." Lucas pauses. "Has she decided if she's going to run the place?"

"She said she'd see how she feels," says Benedict. "But between you and me, she's been bored lately. I saw pictures of that hotel. It looks like shit. You know how she loves a good renovation project."

I put up my hand.

"What?" asks Lucas.

"Who's Leilah?"

"You'll meet her tomorrow night."

"But—"

"Later," says Lucas. "Let Benedict finish."

"What are you doing?" Benedict frowns. "That's not how you raise a newborn. You have to nurture their curiosity and interest in this world they now find themselves in. How else are they going to properly adjust to their new life?"

"I was just saying that the other night," says Henry, who is absolutely full of shit.

"Perhaps if you spent more time talking to her and less time doing whatever it was you were doing on that bed..." The look of much judgment Benedict lays on Lucas makes my night.

Henry nods. "Yeah, Father. Good point, Benedict. Hear, hear."

"You've never even turned anyone, Henry," says Lucas.

"Of course not." Henry wrinkles his nose. "I don't want that kind of responsibility. Ew."

Lucas squeezes his eyelids shut tight with an expression of great pain. I do my best to hold back a smile, but I'm not trying very hard. Watching his own people give him crap is one of the true joys in my new undead life.

"Skye," says Benedict. "The position of enforcer in our family is held by Leilah. She was a seamstress to a Persian princess and was turned in the 1300s."

"Oh, I love this story," says Henry, sitting up straight. "She challenged Father to this game. It was kind of like an early version of backgammon. Whoever won had to grant the other a favor. She, of course, thrashed him, and he had to make her a vampire. Isn't that great?"

Lucas frowns. "She didn't thrash me. I wanted to turn her. The woman has a mind like no other."

"What's the difference between an enforcer and an assassin?" I ask.

"Both of them are Father's boot for kicking ass," says Henry. "They basically do his dirty work. But an enforcer does publicly what an assassin does in secret."

"How big is our family?" I ask. "What even *is* the vampire definition of a family, for that matter?"

"Not as big as some. Lucas is careful in who he turns, and encourages us to be the same," says Benedict. "Our family consists of all those turned by Lucas, and then all of those who we turned, and so on down through the ages."

"What positions do you and Henry hold?"

"He's the court fool," says Benedict.

Henry ignores the insult. "I'm courtier. My job is to deliver Father's messages and negotiate with other families when required."

"But since Lucas was sleeping and Henry was available, he has been working with me as a guard." Benedict scratches at his beard. "Now that Lucas is awake, I am here to watch his back once more, and Henry will return to the job of talking at people."

Henry scowls. "I don't just talk at them. It's more involved than that. Then there's the whole spymaster side of things. I'm a very important person, Benedict."

"Whatever you say, little brother."

"Don't get ahead of yourself," says Lucas. "I still haven't decided if you're taking over as spymaster."

"What happened to the last one?" I ask.

Benedict says nothing, but his gaze jumps to Lucas.

"She was killed, unfortunately." Henry winces. "It's a sad story. Let's talk about it another time."

Lucas says nothing, but his frown game is strong. He stretches an arm out along the back of the couch and starts playing with a lock of my hair. Again. He winds it around one of his fingers and tugs—just a little. It's like I'm his fidget toy or something.

"Do all vampire families work this way?" I ask.

"Not all of them," says Benedict. "Not every vampire wants or needs community. There are loners and nomads out there. The sire bond can be broken."

"There are vampires who just want to vibe." Henry crosses his legs and swings his foot back and forth. "Live and learn and experience things. Not get caught up in all of the politics and wars. What we have is a more traditional model of a family. But it's still common enough. The major families around the world all operate similarly."

"Okay."

"A lot of families break apart due to infighting. Or due to the sire being an overbearing wanker," says Henry. "But Father doesn't tend to impose his will on us in assholish ways. And we actually all quite like each other."

"Yes." Benedict nods. "Mostly."

Henry throws a silk cushion in his face. Of course, Benedict catches it and sets it aside. He rises and heads into the hallway. "I need weapons. They make such a fuss at LAX when I bring them with me."

Henry jumps up to follow. "I'll be interested to hear what you think of the new additions I made to the armory. The man-portable missile, in particular, looks to be an absolute hoot."

"We're in the middle of a city," says Lucas. "You're not firing any missiles, Henry."

"I am just going to pretend I didn't hear that."

"Henry," growls Lucas.

The man sighs heartily. "Yes, Father. Fine. No missiles."

Benedict reaches above the frame of one of the doors in the hallway. With an old key now in hand, he unlocks the door and walks inside.

"The keys were sitting above the doors the entire damn time?" I ask in a not-so-nice tone of voice.

"Yes," says Lucas. "Everyone needs access. This is, after all, a family home."

I have nothing. Absolutely nothing. Also, I am an idiot.

"What's that thing on Father's face?" asks Benedict in his low rumble of a voice.

"I believe it's his attempt at a smile." Henry wanders into a room that can only be described as an armory, and we all follow along behind him. "Terrifying, isn't it?"

It's another large room with stone walls. But these walls are covered in neat racks of killing devices. Daggers, swords, spears, bows and arrows, and so on. There are also shields and various types of armor. In the center of the room are heavy wooden chairs and a large table with brushes and cloths to clean the weapons lined up neatly. Inside a display case is a silver axe with runes etched into the metal. And there are also guns...lots of guns.

Benedict waves a hand at them and says, "But they're so loud and messy and modern."

"I've seen you in a crowd wielding a broadsword, big brother. Now that was loud and messy."

"That was all just a misunderstanding. We laughed about it later."

"The people who still had all of their limbs attached," says Henry. "Sure."

Benedict just sniffs in disdain.

Vampires are violent by nature. I get that. We're less removed from our food source than most humans. And then there's all of the politics and infighting to consider. But this room is a lot. "There are enough weapons in here to start a war."

"Or to end one." Lucas stares at the axe in its case. "But let's hope it doesn't come to that."

# ☾ CHAPTER NINE

I wake up in Lucas's bed again. He's lying on his back with his hands behind his head, staring at the ceiling. No idea what deep thoughts he might be thinking. I must have fallen asleep in the living room, listening to Henry and Benedict telling stories about the past. Despite my repeated requests for a room of my own, Lucas apparently carried me into his. Guess he still doesn't trust me not to run amok. Which is ridiculous. Henry did delight in telling me that the vase I almost broke last night was a first-edition Wedgewood from 1793 worth approximately half a million. But I wouldn't have almost broken it if Lucas hadn't been chasing me in the first place, so there.

My funeral must be any day now. I didn't ask when they were burying fake me from the fire. They might just be putting the ashes in an urn. I don't have any particular preference. Such a sad and horrible time for my family and friends. My heart hurts just thinking about it. No one likes losing a loved one or being reminded of their mortality. I wish I had the photos from my cell and apartment. Anything familiar would be nice. Like my favorite tee or the few pieces of jewelry I treasured. Guess the antique silver locket Mom gave me for my twenty-fifth birthday would be out, even if it hadn't been destroyed by the flames.

Grief is strange. And I am mourning my old life. It's the little things. Like walking to the café down the street on a Sunday morning or receiving random text messages from friends. All of that life is just waiting a short drive from here. But it might as well be on the moon. At least I can still remember Mom's voice and Dad's laugh. Or the way Nicole would roll her eyes when I tried to tell a joke and mangled yet another punchline. And I play those cherished memories over and over inside my mind.

Meanwhile, here I am living in the vampire equivalent of a hobbit hole in the Hollywood Hills with a bunch of immortal male models. The places life takes you. Or death, for that matter.

"I thought about having you stay here at the house tonight," Lucas says out of nowhere. "But it's not the right choice. You need to see how the family works together. You also need to be seen to be fitting in and taking your place."

"You're worried people will see me as a weakness."

Nothing from him.

I roll onto my side, all the better to stare at him. Nothing happens. I screw up my face and concentrate harder.

"Are you trying to read my mind?" he asks with a faint smile.

"It's not working."

"Just ask me what I'm thinking. It might be faster."

"Alright," I say. "What are you thinking?"

"That the situation in L.A. is more complex than I like. But I still consider this city my home. For now, at least." He jerks his chin at the bedside table. "Drink your blood bags. As soon as the sun goes down, we're leaving."

I sit up and stop. Because there on the bedside table, along with my evening blood bags, is an old, red velvet box. "What's this?"

"Just something I found lying around. Thought you might like it."

Inside are two diamond-stud earrings. And they are not small. "Holy shit. That is not nothing. Not even remotely."

"Don't make a big deal out of it. I picked them up in Belgium a while back." His dark brows draw close together. "It's good to diversify investments. Not to have everything tied up in property."

"They're beautiful. The first-edition Austen and now these…I'm beginning to think somewhere down in the depths of your dark and creepy heart, you actually like me, Lucas."

He grunts. "Hurry up and drink your blood. We don't have all night."

I set aside the expensive jewelry and start sucking down the red stuff. "Where are we going and how dangerous is it going to be?"

"It should be straightforward. Archie owned The Boulevard. His family is in disarray so we're claiming the building, along with his seat on the board."

"What happens to any of his people who are still there?"

"We won't hurt anyone who doesn't try to hurt us first. Any of his people still in the building can resettle elsewhere. He's sure to have owned other properties we can use for that purpose." Lucas looks me over. "Skye, do you know how to fire a gun or defend yourself?"

"I hate guns. But I did take a self-defense course when I was eighteen."

"Hang back and keep your head down. Do exactly as you're told at all times," he says. "Am I understood?"

"You're worried about how it's going to go down tonight." I don't need to read minds to know this much. It's obvious from his body language and tone of voice.

"Everything will be fine." And that's all he says.

Benedict drives a bulletproof Mercedes G Wagon. It is every bit as big and built as the man himself. He takes his job as guard seriously. His gaze is constantly on the move once we leave the house, watching for attack. The amount of weaponry he and Henry removed from the armory was wild. However, they wouldn't even let me have a dagger. Not even a reasonably dull letter opener. Which is insulting. I'm wearing another set of black jeans, boots, and a tee. Much the same as the others. And the way Lucas pulls off jeans and a V-neck tee is a sight to be seen. Modern, casual clothing suits him just fine. I ignore Benedict's quiet suggestion to wipe the drool off my chin. One of us has to behave like an adult.

One of these nights I'm going to stop being so mesmerized by Lucas. Any time now. That would be nice.

The diamond earrings are still sitting safe and sound on the bedside table. I don't even know what to think about the gift giving. Nothing about this situation makes sense. And Lucas's reasons for doing things tend to be sketchy at best.

When we pull up outside The Boulevard Hotel, all is eerily quiet. No sign of guests, staff, or others. But the doors are open, and the lights are on. A woman wearing a white pantsuit and heels walks out to greet us. She has brown skin and shoulder-length dark hair with strands of silver. Her chunky, sapphire and white-gold necklace is stunning. So, too, is the matching dagger she carries on her hip. There's nothing low key about this woman. She's living forever in high style.

"You just couldn't stay home and leave this to me, could you?" she asks in a husky voice with an accent. "Why am I not surprised?"

Lucas gives her a warm smile. "Leilah."

"Hello, old man. It's been a while." She nods to each of us in turn, giving me a curious glance. "Welcome to the family, sister."

"Thank you."

"Come on then, let's get this done," she says, turning back to the building. "My people have already started on the belowground levels. Any stragglers we find will be held down in the bar for questioning. Why don't we work our way up?"

We take the stairs. The hotel has sixty rooms and suites, and all of them need to be cleared. Along with the ballroom, restaurant, and so on. The same air of neglect is evident on other levels. Stale air and marks on the walls. Worn carpet and battered furniture. I would give this place two stars at most. As we were told, Archie's family seems to have fled. The hotel seems empty. Almost.

My job is to listen at the door for any signs of life, then throw it open and stay back while Henry rushes through the room like a hurricane. Once the room has been declared clear, we move on to the next. Lucas isn't a fan of me doing even this much. Though, I get the distinct feeling my job has been invented just for me. That Henry wanted me to feel included. But whatever. I am fine with letting the others go hard core.

Being given safe duties does nothing to stop me from being strung out from head to toe. And I break a good three door handles before getting myself under control. All while Lucas gives me side-eye. So not helpful.

We find a terrified vampire hiding on the third floor. The word *Woodsman* surrounded by fear appears inside my head. When Lucas makes no move to harm them, they seem confused. Henry shepherds them down to the bar in the basement. Nothing else happens on the third floor.

But one hiding on the fourth floor opens fire on us with some sort of pistol. The pop of the silenced gun is horrible to hear. All too reminiscent of being fired at outside the nightclub.

Lucas is covering me and pushing me down when the first bullet flies over my head. One moment I am standing, the next I've face-planted on the floor. Which gets me out of the line of fire, thank fuck.

Then Lucas appears farther down the hallway with another heart in his fist a moment later. There wasn't even time for me to react. Benedict just offers me a hand and sighs as if he's upset that he hasn't gotten to rip out anyone's internal organs. He might be the guard, but telling Lucas to hang back and keep safe would be a waste of time. The vampire does what he wants.

Benedict inspects the splintered wall. "Wooden bullets again."

Lucas's gaze is searing. The heart turns to ash in his hand as he strides back down the hallway. "Skye, were you hit?"

"No."

"Are you sure?"

"Yes."

"There's no scent of blood," says Benedict. "Not on her."

Lucas's jawline is set in harsh lines. Like the man is internalizing a whole lot of anger.

It's a struggle to keep my expression cool and calm. Because if he hadn't been by my side, I would be dead. Deader. However, this situation is already intense, and the last thing anyone needs is me freaking out just because it's the second time someone has tried to kill me since I became a blood sucker.

We move carefully through the rest of the floor without any further mishap. Out of the seven floors aboveground, only the top two seem to have been used by Archie's family. As evidenced by the covered windows and the scattered and abandoned clothes and other possessions. It looks like they left in a hurry. Guess the other five levels were reserved for actual guests. Imagine what the reviews for this place would be like. Who would want to stay at a rundown hotel where you were as likely to wind up on the menu as you were to get a good night's sleep?

While Henry has chosen not to turn anyone, Leilah has apparently made herself an undead army. Over a dozen of her people swarm the building. Guess they count as extended family now. They range in race, age, and gender. Some wear tactical gear, while others are in street clothes like us. Each and every one of them seem to know exactly what they're doing. The way they watch Lucas with a mixture of awe and wariness is interesting. It's like he's a god walking among mortals.

We encounter more problems on the sixth floor. There's a loud bang, then the walls shake. Dust and paint flakes rain down on all of us. And one of Leilah's people is immediately reduced to ash by the explosion.

"Dammit, Fionn. You foolish boy. Always fucking rushing," hisses Leilah. No one says anything as she takes a moment to collect herself before announcing, "Be careful. They've set breach charges. Where's Margaret?"

"Coming." A striking woman with white skin and gray hair joins us in the hallway. She's older than Leilah and has an upper-class English accent. "Excuse me."

"She's human," I whisper.

Lucas turns to me. "Skye, have you got yourself under control?"

Her blood is calling to me. The familiar whooshing sound of it rushing through her veins and the steady beat of her heart are like a symphony. And I am more than aware of it, being so close. But there are none of the shakes and watering-mouth business. "Yes."

"Margaret is Leilah's paramour. She's also a witch," supplies Henry. "Biting her is not something I would suggest trying. A very good way to get yourself slapped down, sister."

"When did that start?" asks Lucas.

"1969. They met at Woodstock. You know, that great concert I told you about outside New York where everyone was all free love and dropping acid?"

Lucas nods.

Safe to say I am no longer permitted to open any doors. Margaret mutters something and walks slowly forward with one hand raised. A faint clicking noise can be heard behind several of the doors lining the hallway as she passes. But nothing else goes boom. Thank goodness. She doesn't look like your stereotypical witch. There's no dramatic pointed hat or such. Just jeans and a flowing white top. A collection of silver chains and crystals hang around her neck. But it's a chunk of clear quartz that she holds in her hand while moving forward and dealing with the explosive devices.

There's an event space on the sixth floor. Guess it gave the guests a nice view of the city. And behind those large doors I can feel something. A lot of thoughts and feelings, and the dominant ones are anger and fear.

"There are people in there," I say. "They're angry and afraid."

"That's all you're getting?" asks Lucas.

"Yeah."

Leilah stares at me for a moment before flicking her wrist. Four of her people step forward and they're all armed to the teeth. Guns and daggers and you name it. But then so are Henry and Benedict. Lucas is the only one who seems to prefer using his own two hands. Everyone else waits in silence to see what happens next.

"Throw aside your weapons and lie face down on the floor with your hands on your head," yells Leilah. "Any creature not in this position when we enter will be destroyed. This is your only warning. You do not need to suffer the final death tonight."

After a moment, she gives her people a nod. The four blur and enter the room. Next comes the sounds of gunfire and screaming. *Shit*. The whole situation makes my skin crawl. But I do my best to keep my thoughts and feelings from showing on my face. The silence that follows the violence feels almost as bad.

Leilah pulls a cell out of her jacket pocket and reads the screen. "Lucas, you're wanted down in the basement bar. We can finish up here."

He nods, puts a hand to the small of my back, and leads us toward the elevators. Benedict follows close behind. Henry never came back up after shepherding the vampire down to the speakeasy. And they're not the only ones down there. A good fifteen members of Archie's family are sitting at the tables with worried faces. They're guarded by a couple of Leilah's people.

Lucas walks past them and straight into the board meeting room at the back of the premises. It's as dark and creepy as the other night. But this time, a vampire with white skin and short red hair wearing a Lakers tee is tied to one of the board members' chairs—with a dagger sticking out of each of his thighs and another embedded in his stomach.

Ouch. Given how fast we heel, the skin and flesh must now be sticking to those blades. So much blood. But not human. I can definitely smell the difference. Body parts and various liquids must only turn to ash once the vampire in question is dead.

How the hell is this my life now?

"Father," says Henry with a bright smile. "This is Josh. We were just playing a game with him, which we were all enjoying immensely, weren't we?"

Another vampire leans against a nearby wall with a dagger in his hand. He's tall with a lean, muscular build and shoulder-length, dark hair. There is dried blood and the lingering pink line of a healing cut on his arm. Along with a fading gray bruise on his jawline. While he has the same coloring as Lucas, he has a more disheveled air. There's none of the slicked-back hair and freshly shaven face. This man is handsome in an unkempt way, and was also turned around the age of forty, at a guess.

"Nico, he cut you?" asks Lucas. "Have you slowed down since I've been asleep?"

The vampire smiles. "This one was Archie's assassin. He has some skills. I found him in the bottom parking lot trying to escape. This place is riddled with tunnels and secret rooms."

"How interesting. He was his assassin, and yet he chose not to come after me himself. Instead, sending someone to attempt a drive-by shooting." Lucas wanders over to the bound man and pulls out one of the daggers. "Why is that, exactly?"

Josh's eyes widen in pain, but his mouth stays shut.

Nico lets the knife in his hand fly. It finds its target in the captive's shoulder, and Josh's whole body jerks. "Honestly," says Nico, "I think this asshole just lacked the courage to go after the Woodsman himself."

Lucas glances at Henry, giving him the go ahead.

"Alrighty," he says, sitting on the stately board table, which I highly doubt is allowed. "Here's how this is going to go, Josh. We've been having fun playing up until now, but as you can see, Father has arrived. Therefore, it's time to get down to business. Either you answer our questions or—"

"You're going to kill me anyway," groans Josh.

"I can't believe you interrupted me. That is so fucking rude." Henry flicks his blond hair back. I've never seen a courtier in action before, but this is interesting. "And, duh. You had a marksman fire on Father and his new favorite. Do you have any idea how long we've all been hoping he'd get himself a special someone? Centuries, dude. Centuries. And then you come along and try to kill her, too."

Nothing from Josh.

Though, Lucas now has a muscle twitching in his jawline. Has to be from irritation. In a feat of supernatural strength, I, myself, manage to not smack Henry upside the head. And the way Nico is giving me the once-over with his cool gaze is unnecessary, and not particularly brotherly or comfortable.

"So, of course, we're going to kill you," continues Henry. "But it's how you die that's up for discussion."

Josh does not look convinced.

"Here's what's going to happen. Our family assassin, Nicholas, is going to start cutting pieces off you. Fingers and toes and then limbs and so on. He'll just sort of work his way inward. It's his specialty. You'd be amazed how long he can keep you alive while dismembering you. And you will talk. Through it all. They all do eventually."

Josh sneers. "I'm not even the real fucking threat to you people."

"Is that so?" asks Henry. "Do tell."

"If you don't kill me, he will. He gave me the money to hire the shooter. I'm fucked either way without Archie to protect me."

"Archie gave you the money?"

The man shakes his head and grimaces. "No."

"Who gave you the money and will kill you, Josh?" asks Lucas.

"He's been with the Russians for centuries. Who do you think whispered in Lev's ear about how L.A. would be the perfect choice for a new hunting ground?" asks Josh. "None of the families here knew how to work together before Lev tried to take over. The city was chaos. Just ready and waiting for them to seize control. But it was all really a cover for him to fuck with you and yours."

"We need a name, Josh," says Henry.

Josh spits a gob of blood at my feet. The way the asshole then grins at me is gross...remnants of crimson covering his lips and teeth. "And he wants *her* bad. You should hear him. He saw the security footage from the other night when you killed Archie. I don't know what it is about her, but the sight of that one at your side sent him into a frenzy."

My whole body goes rigid.

"Who?" asks Lucas in a deadly tone.

"Your brother." Josh laughs maniacally. "You fucked up, Woodsman. He's still alive."

# ☾ CHAPTER TEN

There's a car on fire parked on the street outside the house when we return. Tonight could not get any stranger if it tried. Flames reach high into the sky as the red lights of a fire engine go round and round. But the firefighters have it under control quickly. So many nosy neighbors huddled nearby. Seems like the whole street is out there. Coming home to a fire is not so welcoming. And since when did I start thinking of this place as home?

"What now?" asks Henry with a groan.

"See what you can find out," says Lucas.

Henry is out of the vehicle and striding toward the authorities with a confident smile in place before we've come to a complete stop. Benedict then drives on into the garage with a pistol sitting in his lap. Everyone is on edge.

"They could have attempted to blow up the upper levels of the house if they really tried," says Lucas. "I don't know for sure if the runes would stop a fire up there. But whoever it is, they're just messing with us."

"I assume this is more bullshit from your brother to keep us busy," says Benedict.

"Seems likely."

"Are we relocating?"

Lucas shakes his head. "No. The other properties don't have the same protections as this one, and it probably wouldn't take long to track us. Let's stay put for now."

Benedict just nods.

I, on the other hand, have some questions. "What if someone does blow up the upper levels? Do we just die horribly underneath the rubble or what?"

"The runes will protect us down there," says Lucas. "And rest assured, there's more than one way out of there in case of an emergency."

"Any particular reason why your brother would want to kill you," I ask, climbing out of the car and following him through the house and down to the basement level.

"It's complicated." Lucas scowls. "But the last time I saw Marc, he was bleeding out on the floor with a selection of my favorite daggers in his back. I also poured gasoline over him and set the building on fire that he was in. If he did survive, I would like to know how."

"We need to talk," I say.

"I'm aware," answers Lucas. "Benedict, get me an update on what's happening in the city. If there's been any sightings of Lev or his people. Henry will also have connections."

Benedict nods. "When do you want to deal with—"

"Later," says Lucas, cutting him off.

The big blond dude heads into the armory. He and Henry had a couple of laptops set up on the table in there earlier. Guess it's their new HQ.

"This way." Lucas leads me down the hallway of the underground lair. He retrieves the key from atop the frame and unlocks a door. "After you."

It's another room I haven't been in before. Inside is an office with a large, ornate mahogany desk and matching chair. Three walls are taken up with more books and curios. The man is seriously such a hoarder. And on the last wall is a chipped and faded painting of a woman.

I can definitely see the resemblance. She has blonde hair, green eyes, and the same soft curves as me. The same heavy jawline, full lips, and direct gaze. Huh.

"You did well tonight." Lucas shuts the door and leans his back against it. "Though, you still seem pretty wound up. We should do something about that."

I nod to the painting. "Tell me about her."

"Her name was Ana, and she was my brother's wife," he says. "It was an arranged marriage. He was the oldest son and heir, but I was known for my skill at hunting. It gave me an excuse to spend most of my time in the hills. A man was attacked in our village, and I was given the task of tracking the creature responsible. It turned out to be a vampire. He was impressed with my skills and decided to turn me. And I then offered to turn Ana."

"But not your brother?"

"No," says Lucas. "Marc has always been an ass. I had no interest in spending eternity in his company. But I had feelings for Ana."

"Were they reciprocated?"

"Yes. But she held sacred the marriage vows she had made to my brother. Nothing happened between us. I knew she wouldn't agree to be turned. She had children who needed her. My brother was often busy elsewhere, and she enjoyed much of the simple life she lived."

I sit in the seat behind the desk and cross my legs. "Okay."

"A year later she died in childbirth. But not before my brother had gotten the story out of her about how I'd been made into a vampire and offered to make her one, too." Lucas crosses his arms. "Finding out I had feelings for his wife... let's just say, he didn't take the news well. Marc searched for a vampire who would turn him and eventually found one. But he wasn't as strong as me, and he knew it. The one who turned him was only a few years old; whereas, my sire was ancient. The bubonic plague killed most of what remained of our human family soon after. The truth is, Marc was my last real link to that life, and I was reluctant to destroy it. Pure sentiment on my part. Every century or so he made a halfhearted attempt to kill me, but it was almost a game between us."

"You think someone trying to kill you is a game?"

He sighs. "You have to understand, he had much the same number of years as me to become an expert at whatever he pleased. I know he spent time learning fighting from the Huns and the Knights Templar. Had he been fully determined to kill me for falling in love with his wife, I would have known."

I frown.

"Then in 1955, he killed my spymaster, Meriwa. I had asked everyone to stay away from him. But she didn't like loose ends and wanted to keep better track of his movements. Not to kill him, you understand, but just to know where he was and what he was planning. He sent her ashes back to me in a silver chest. She had been part of our family for four-hundred years. That's when I decided the time had finally come to end my brother."

"And that's why you went to sleep?"

"Their deaths weighed on me for various reasons. It would seem I was premature in mourning my brother, however." He watches me in silence for a moment, before saying, "After Ana broke my dark and creepy heart, as you called it, I tended to steer clear of anyone who reminded me of her. Until you. I won't let him hurt you, Skye."

"When did all of this start between you and your brother?"

"Arthur had just defeated the Saxons at the Battle of Badon."

"Wait. King Arthur? I thought he wasn't real."

He shrugs. "The mythology surrounding him is mostly nonsense, but the man himself was real enough."

"What year was it?"

His lips skew to the side in annoyance. The dude definitely has hang-ups about his age. "Around the start of the sixth century."

"You're, um, fifteen-hundred years old?"

"Give or take."

"You are one-thousand-and-five-hundred years old. Approximately. And you've been carrying that picture of her around the entire time. That's either dedication or taking the idea of emotional baggage way too far." My eyes must be as wide as the moon. "But you know I'm not her."

"Oh, I know. Ana was soft-spoken. You have yet to have a thought cross your mind that you don't believe needs announcing."

"You really think you're the first person to tell me I'm too loud or too much?" I ask with a bitter smile.

His gaze turns hard. "Who said that to you?"

Ignoring his question, I ask one of my own. "Why did you really turn me?"

"Who insulted you in such a manner, Skye? I want their name."

"It doesn't matter. Not anymore," I say. "Answer the question. Why did you turn me?"

"I've already given you my reasons for that."

"Let's revisit them just once more for old time's sake," I say, picking up a heavy gold fountain pen off the desk. It's tempting to throw it at him, but he would only catch it. "I reminded you of your first love."

"For a moment. Yes. But the reason I turned you, Skye, was because neither Henry nor Benedict were where they were supposed to be. I woke up in a new century I didn't understand. I knew you'd be useful in helping me adapt."

I snort.

"Were you hoping for more?"

"No."

"Very well then. We've covered the reason why I turned you." He cocks his head. "But would you like to know why you're still sleeping in my bed?"

"Because you don't trust me on my own, along with the added bonus that you know it annoys me. You'd think pettiness fades with age, but apparently not." I toss the heavy pen back onto the desk and get to my feet. "We're done here. Thanks for finally telling me what's going on. Move, please."

Lucas stays put with his back to the door. "Make me."

"I'm not in the mood to play."

"That's a pity, because I am."

"Then go find Monica," I say.

And the moment the words are out of my mouth, I know they're a mistake.

"Who?" His dark brows draw together. "You mean the human I drank from the other night? The one on Henry's payroll?"

"Henry really pays her?"

"Some are willing to sell their blood." He gazes down at me with curiosity. "You're jealous. But I was barely with her long enough to feed. Why be jealous?"

"I am not jealous."

"Yes, you are. But all of your emotions are heightened right now. And since I'm your sire, it's normal to feel drawn to me. It's not usually something I encourage, but in your case, I've decided to make an exception."

"Ha. No. Don't do me any favors."

"Come here," he orders.

I feel the corresponding tug inside my chest. And it's not like I didn't ask him not to use the compulsion crap on me. "Fuck you."

His smile has more than a flash of fang. "Fuck me yourself, you coward."

"Great. You've discovered memes." And I kind of hate myself for asking, but I really want to know. "Are you still in love with Ana?"

"No. Of course not. She was a good woman. But she's been dead for over a millennia. Now come here."

I shake my head and go to take a step back. But he moves forward and grabs the armholes on the front of my tank, including the lace bra straps beneath. I push against his rock-hard chest and get approximately nowhere. "Let go of me."

"No. Never," he says adamantly. "Especially when that's not what you really want."

"Like you know what I want. You are such a—"

Suddenly he's moved us and reversed our positions. My back is hard against the door. As much as I'd like to knee him in the balls, he's maneuvered us so that his booted feet are between mine. His body is pressing against mine from knees to chest. All I can do is push at his chest or grip his arms, and neither move does a damn thing.

He pushes his face into the side of my neck and breathes deep, making me shiver. And I hate the way I react to him. It isn't fair—a childish statement, but true nonetheless.

"I'm such a what?" he asks, calm as can be.

"I don't know. But if you start going on about my scent again..."

"Why do you keep not finishing sentences?" he asks. "It shows a real lack of commitment on your part."

If my heart still worked, it would be racing. I growl in frustration and the bastard actually laughs. Then he drags the flat of his tongue up my neck. Which shouldn't turn me on. But I am now a mass of nerves, and every damn last one of them is titillated by the jerk. Dammit. All of this tension simmers inside of me, pushing me to fuck, or fight, or I don't know what.

The backs of his fingers move restlessly against my skin, where he's still got ahold of my tank and bra. "All the times I have thought of you with your hand between your sweet thighs," he says.

"You don't need to be thinking about that. It has nothing to do with you."

"But it's not enough for you, is it?" he asks. "You need me."

"The ego on you...holy shit."

"You don't just smell good, Skye, you taste good, too. Yours was the sweetest blood I've ever had. I think it's time you took your clothes off."

I bark out a nervous laugh. "Absolutely not."

"Why not?"

"You don't want to have sex with me. You said so. What happened to a newborn's infatuation being a horrible inconvenience and all that?"

"Like I said, I changed my mind."

"Change it back again. I'll wait."

"I tried, you know," he says. "I attempted to convince myself this infatuation with you was foolish. But it didn't work."

"It's only been a few days. Try harder."

"No. Be as angry as you like. I am, without a doubt, the most selfish creature walking the face of this Earth. Because no matter what is best, I refuse to give you up. Having you with me, keeping you close, it makes me happy."

I screw up my nose. "It makes you what?"

"Henry explained to me how obsessed people are with the search for happiness in these modern times. I am surprised to find I agree. Duty, loyalty...they don't often keep you warm at night. But you, my dear Skye, do."

Without another word, he tears the front of my tank in half right down the middle. The pads of his fingers glide over the lace of my bra, his thumbs toying with the hard imprint of my nipples. The way he rests his forehead against mine, keeping us as close as can be. Shit. This is not good.

What is also not good is the way everything low in my belly has drawn tight. How the crotch of my panties is wet with need. It makes it hard to remember how much I kind of, maybe mostly, hate the man. At least, I think I should?

"I miss the days when women wore skirts all of the time," he says. "You're going to make getting those boots and pants off you a chore, aren't you?"

"Lucas..."

"And there you go, starting a thought and not finishing it again. It's turning into a habit." His hands cup my breasts over the lace of my bra. The hardening length of his cock presses against me, making me squirm. And there's no way he hasn't noticed. "I have just one question for you, Skye."

"What?"

He grips the back of my neck and kisses me hard. His tongue sliding straight in and taking me over. The way he pushes his mouth against mine is punishing in its intensity. I hate the way he goes straight to my head and lights up my body from top to toe. Never in my life has anyone had such an effect on me.

When he draws back to look me over, to take in my reaction to him, it's with a self-satisfied smile. I despise how damn pleased he is with himself.

He winds a lock of my blonde hair around his finger, and that's when I see it over his shoulder. The painting of Ana. She stares vacantly out from the canvas with her golden hair, green eyes, and vapid expression.

And I refuse to be a poor imitation of some dead chick he pined after way back when.

No longer am I a mixture of confused and turned on. Now, I am also righteously angry.

He might have a point about my emotions being heightened. I have never hit anyone in my life. But I barely stop to think it through before slapping him hard across his perfect face. A violent red outline of my hand appears on his cheek before fading away.

"What was that for?" he asks in his annoyingly calm tone.

"I am not Ana."

"No," he agrees. "You're not. Didn't we already discuss that?"

Before I can open the door and make my escape, he's reversed our positions again. The door is at his back, he's guarding the only exit, and I am caught once more between him and the desk. "I am not your toy to play with. Whatever your reasons."

"We might have to agree to disagree about that."

"Shut up and listen. I may not be able to deny a certain attraction between us. But it is absolutely not going any further. For so very many reasons, but especially not so long as you have that damn painting of her on the wall."

"You want me to take down the painting?"

"Yes. Now get out of the way."

He shakes his head. "No."

"No?"

"You heard me."

The violence this man brings out in me. How dare he order me around and put his hands on me. Never has someone bossed me around and turned me on in equal measure. I don't like feeling this out of control.

It wouldn't be an overstatement to say I have no idea what I am doing. Not really. But it doesn't stop me, let alone slow me down. My rage doesn't have time for reason. I fly at the man, and he catches me with ease. I might want to learn how to fight before trying to take on Lucas. Ask Benedict for some lessons or something. It would probably be the smart thing to do if I wanted an actual chance in Hell against this particular fifteen-hundred-year-old vampire.

An attempt at biting him soon turns into us kissing. Again. Our tongues tangle furiously, and my teeth sink into his bottom lip. The way his grip on me tightens, holding me to him. I think I understand now why he keeps sniffing me. Because his masculine scent is otherworldly. A hint of salt and sandalwood and I don't know what.

I shred the material of his tee, tearing it from his body, needing to be skin to skin. The seductive smile he gives me in return makes my knees quiver.

The next thing I know, my back hits the desktop and my boots, socks, and jeans are gone. Just gone. Same for the remains of my torn tank top. He is amazingly adept at destroying clothing. My lips are numb and swollen from kissing, and my head spins in dizzy circles. I can't keep up. But the way my pussy clenches at the sight of him half naked cannot be denied. The way all of the smooth skin of his chest is on show. His wide shoulders and muscular neck, in particular, make me stupid with lust. He says I am his weakness, but he is also mine. That's the truth of the matter.

"I like the lingerie of this time." He stands at the end of the desk, gazing down on me. At my black lace Brazilian brief. His palms glide over my thick thighs, holding them apart. "You can keep the bra. For now."

"Lucas, wait," I say. But I might as well have saved my words.

He tears my underwear from my body and drags me farther down the desk. Closer to him. Then his face is buried in my pussy.

# BECAUSE THE NIGHT

I hadn't given much thought to vampire sex. But it is definitely something to be experienced. His stamina and strength are unmatched. Guess you can learn a lot about anatomy in a thousand or so years. He drags the flat of his tongue through me, over and over again. Then he suckles at my labia, giving me just the right amount of pressure. The decadent, wet sounds of him eating me are obscene. Same goes for my moans.

My hands find his thick hair and hold on tight. The way he grinds his face against my sex is wild. How his thumbs hold me open, as he fucks me with his tongue. No man has ever come at me with such raw enthusiasm.

It's mildly embarrassing how quickly he makes me come. How fast the sensation builds down low in my spine before shooting out to every part of me. He sucks on my clitoris and slides two fingers into me. And those digits faithfully find their target. My mind goes into freefall as the orgasm consumes me. All of me drawing tight before unraveling. I am stardust. I am gone. What remains of me is floating in the heavens high above.

He moves me back up the desk and I barely notice. It takes a while for my mind to come down. For me to put myself back together. But when I do, it's to the sight of his body covering me. His jeans are pushed down, he's positioned between my legs, and oh wow. We are really doing this.

"Do you want me inside you?" he asks.

"Yes."

With one hard thrust, he buries himself deep. And there's a lot of him.

A squeak of surprise escapes my throat. The length is blissfully fine, but the width requires a moment to adjust.

His face is stark with need, his gaze glued to mine as he holds perfectly still. My mouth opens, but nothing comes out. I officially have no words—which might be a first.

He nods. Happy with whatever he sees in my expression. One hand has a tight grip on my hair while the other has an equally firm grip on an ass cheek. He's in the perfect position to do as he wants with me. And that is exactly what he does. Lucas fucks me with brutal efficiency. I have to wrap my legs around his waist and grip the sides of the desk to stop him from driving us both off the damn end and onto the floor.

His hips piston, burying his hard length deep, time and again. My hard nipples rub against his strong chest through the lace of my bra. The way the delicious friction is building me right back up again is almost sinful. Coming twice in one night has happened to me approximately never. Not with someone else involved. But the blood is rushing through me, hot and sweet. The pressure is gathering in a tight ball low in my belly and back. All of me is focused on the knot of tension between my hips.

The blue of his eyes is my whole world—the beginning, the end, and everything after. It's like I am lost, and it doesn't even occur to me to care.

I know he's getting close when he presses his face into my neck. A sign that he can't control himself for much longer. Which is fair enough. He hasn't had sex in over seventy years. His grip on my ass tightens and he lifts me just a little. Just enough to have the wide, blunt head of his cock start hitting a beautiful spot deep inside of me. Making me light up from top to toe.

When it comes to fucking, the man is magic. No joke. Never have I been so thoroughly railed. Being with Lucas is like an out-of-body experience.

The sound of wood cracking and splintering as I come is loud. My heart is stuck in my throat, and all I can manage is a moan. But my internal muscles lock on him, trying to keep him deep. The feeling of coming with him inside me is just so sweet and strong.

His roar as he comes echoes through the room. Maybe the whole damn house. That noise shakes my soul, I have never heard anything like it. His hips buck against me a couple of times before he finally stills. For a while, his eyelids remain shut tight, but eventually he opens them.

And we stare at each other warily for a good long time. Completely awkward as fuck.

## CHAPTER ELEVEN

"You once banned me from your office for a decade for daring to sit on the edge of your desk," says Henry. "What Skye just did was much worse."

We're gathered in the living room. I grabbed a fresh tee to wear, but Lucas didn't bother. The reason why soon became obvious. He sits in his throne-like black wingback while Benedict sits on a stool to the side. With a blade and a pair of needle-nose pliers, he goes about the business of digging a bullet out of Lucas' shoulder. As you do. The chandelier has even been turned on for the sake of the surgery, the crystals dazzling in their beauty. I do my best to stare at it instead of the gory display occurring nearby.

Life sure comes at you fast some nights. Honestly.

"She tore off the decorative, hand-carved mahogany siding," the blond idiot continues. "Just crushed it into splinters."

"Shut up, Henry," says Lucas with a wince.

"You need to sit still," grumbles Benedict.

Henry holds up his hands all innocent like. "I'm just saying. The favoritism is starting to get a little bit out of control."

And as for me, I am frowning my heart out. The good vibes from coming hard enough to see whole constellations are long gone. Given Lucas had been tearing out hearts and torturing people, it's not like I would have noticed a little blood and ash on the man. But it is fair to say that Lucas walking around with a bullet in his body since we were fired on in the hallway at the start of the night is freaking me right the fuck out.

The fact that he got shot while protecting me is also taking a moment to process. He stood in front of me and took a bullet. I don't know what to do with the information. How to feel about all of this. "Why didn't you tell me you were hurt?"

"We had more pressing issues to attend to," says Lucas, calm as always.

"You had a bullet in you. What if I had grabbed hold of your shoulder or something?"

"I probably would have mentioned it then."

"Be still." Benedict roots around with the pliers. So gross. Our advanced healing means the skin and flesh keep adhering to the tools. He carefully starts pulling the pliers free of the messy wound. "There we go. It is all in one piece."

Lucas sneers in disdain at the blood-covered wooden bullet.

"It's a whole new level of kink, really." Henry shakes his head in wonder. "Having sex with a bullet lodged in your shoulder. Your strength and tolerance for pain are ridiculous, Father."

"I would have cried like a baby," says the Viking. "It would not be appealing for a lover to see."

"Oh, me, too," agrees Henry. "But I, for one, salute the way Father's thirst overcame his common sense."

"My thirst?" asks Lucas.

"Your yearning, shall we say, for our darling Skye."

"Ah," says Lucas with understanding. "Shut up, Henry."

I sit in the corner of the Chesterfield hugging a cushion to my chest. My human family always gave each other a certain amount of space. My undead family, however, do not. They're happily all up in each other's business. It's going to take some getting used to.

I don't intend on having sex with Lucas again anytime soon. Even though it was amazing. It just wouldn't be a good idea. Our relationship is complicated enough. And there's no reason why a hookup between him and me should be a big deal. Just because it was the best sex I've ever had. This is definitely one of those situations where we did it once to get it out of our systems, and the weird attraction between us is over now.

"You should feed," says Benedict.

"Do you want me to call Monica?" asks Henry.

Lucas's gaze shifts to my face. "No," he says.

Henry looks between us with interest. "If gender is an issue, for some mysterious reason we won't get into, my yoga instructor Gustav lives nearby. Now, he takes the 'body as a temple' idea seriously. His blood is as clean eating as you can get. Or there's the delightful Dylan to consider. They're an artist from Silver Lake. I find the lingering scents of charcoal and oil paint on skin so soothing for some reason. But that might just be me."

Lucas says nothing but gives me definite side-eye. Which isn't wildly suspicious at all.

"I don't understand what's going on," says Benedict.

"It's relationship stuff," answers Henry. "I'll explain later."

And now they're all looking at me. Great. "It's none of my business who you feed from."

Lucas gives me another long look before asking, "Would you be so kind as to fetch me a blood bag, Skye?"

"Sure."

"Here's another new word for you, Father." Henry bites back a smile. "Simp."

I say nothing and head for the kitchen upstairs. Getting away from the three of them for a moment sounds like a damn good idea.

Nothing is going on with Lucas and me. The events of the last half hour were an aberration. It was just sex. Sex that has left me feeling better than I ever have. As if pure energy had been poured through my veins. And yet I am more relaxed than I would have thought possible.

It's probably just a vampire thing and not Lucas-specific, however. He doesn't have a magic dick. Nor is he emotionally available. (The hot ones never are. Though, to be fair. the rest of them usually aren't either.) I also do not need a partner who bosses me around all the time. Not to mention the rather extreme age gap between us. So there's no need for anyone to get carried away and start dreaming of a happy ever after.

The rest of the house is quiet and dark. Though, I can see just fine care of my vampire night vision. My own thirst (for blood) has been easier to manage tonight. But I grab a bag for me out of the fridge, too.

Through the kitchen window, something moves in the garden, out beyond the courtyard. It is as if a shadow coalesces out of nowhere.

And there, staring back at me, is a vaguely familiar man. He wears a button-down shirt beneath a charcoal gray suit.

The white of his shirt seems to glow in the dark shadows at the back of the garden. He isn't even trying to hide. Silver hair cut short, and a face lined with age.

Lucas said it took his brother a while to find a vampire to turn him. It would account for the difference in ages. Marc makes a handsome and commanding figure. Though, perhaps that is down to the similarity in bone structure between the two brothers.

His fine lips curve into a welcoming smile at the sight of me, and his gaze softens as he takes in my face. But the word *Ana* appears inside my head, surrounded by rage. Pure, blood-boiling fury. Without a doubt, this creature would tear me limb from limb given the chance.

He lifts his hand and motions to me to come. As if I would be so stupid.

"I never thought to look on that sweet face again," he says. "How like her you are."

"I'm not Ana."

"He has told you of her then. Good. That's good. And do you know my name?"

"You're Marc."

"That's right." He nods. "Come outside. There is no need for this distance between us while we converse."

"You can't come any closer because of the runes, can you?"

His smile slips. "No. I cannot."

"That must be irritating."

"Very." He frowns. "However, hurting you is not my priority."

"It's not your priority? Oh, that makes me feel so much better. Thanks."

He can't come inside. I am safe for now. But it's not as big a relief as it should be. Because the way he watches me with such ownership and entitlement is beyond creepy. Not even Archie harbored such hatred of me. And he definitely wanted to rip out my heart and eat it—or something.

"Lucas," I say, my voice shaking. "I need you."

A second later, he is standing at my side. Thank goodness. He, too, stares out at the intruder in the garden, his nostrils flaring with anger at the sight. "Hello, brother. It's been a while."

"You shouldn't have made her," says Marc in a low, angry voice.

"She has nothing to do with this."

Marc scoffs. "She has everything to do with this. Ana was my wife. Mine. But even now you cannot accept that. How dare you try to duplicate her with the cheap whore standing at your side."

"Excuse you," I say. "There is nothing wrong with working in the sex trade, or liking sex, for that matter. And I am not cheap."

"That's true," agrees Lucas. "She's really not."

Marc's hands curl into fists. "I could have forgiven you for stabbing me in the back and setting me on fire. It's not as if we haven't had our fun with each other over the years. But not this."

I cock my head. "You could forgive him for stabbing you in the back and setting you on fire? What the fuck is wrong with you people?"

Lucas hushes me before turning back to his brother and saying, "As wonderful as this family reunion has been...what do you want, Marc?"

His brother's answering smile is all sharp teeth. "I will not allow you to use this woman as a weapon against me."

"Are you here on personal business, or are you representing the interests of your Russian friends?"

"Such bitter irony," says Marc. "This situation was years in the making. It took patience to infiltrate The Thorn Group. Then we compelled Jennifer to avoid mentioning that visitors should stay out of the basement when she sent her underling to check the property so close to sunset. I was confident whoever it was she sent would get past the runes and wake you. After all, they would be an innocent who bore you no ill will, and no vampire had actually compelled them. None of us even knew who exactly it would be."

"You did that?" I ask in surprise. "You're the asshole responsible for getting me killed?"

Marc snarls in my general direction. The dude really does not like me. "That she would turn out to look so similar to Ana. And it was me who unknowingly sent her to you."

"Why did you want me woken so badly?" asks Lucas. "Just out of curiosity."

"I look forward to sending you her ashes, brother. The box has already been purchased. Mahogany with gold and pearl inlay. It's quite a fetching piece. Soon." And with that, Marc does a mocking little bow, and then he's gone.

"That's the...actually, I'm not sure how many times it's been now that someone has threatened to kill me," I say. "Do you think he'd feel differently if he got to know me?"

"No. Are you alright?"

I sigh. "I don't know."

He just watches me.

"At least now we know a bit more about what the hell is going on. Shame he wouldn't share his whole nefarious plan with us."

"It would have been helpful."

"How does it feel to have beef going back to the dark ages?" I hand him a blood bag. The way he cringes like a big baby at the thing. "So don't drink it," I say. "It's not like I'm forcing you."

"It's fine," he says, sucking it down with a not-quite-hidden grimace. "Let's head back downstairs."

My jaw cracks on a yawn. "It must be close to dawn."

"Time for you to rest."

"I hate this. I hate being scared. Life would have been a lot nicer if I never knew exactly how many monsters were out there hiding in the dark." I frown. "What have we got on for tomorrow night? More bedlam? Maybe with a side of carnage?"

"I'm not sure yet." His blank face is now impenetrable. I don't have a clue what he is thinking. "You're handling all of this better than I expected. Clearing the hotel. Getting threatened by my brother. Finding out he set you on this course."

"I'm going to pretend that was a compliment."

"It basically was. I will protect you, you know that," he says. "About what happened in my office. I think—"

"Nothing happened in your office. Nothing that we need to discuss, at any rate."

He just looks at me.

"You can relax, Lucas. I'm not going to start clinging to you like some lovestruck baby vampire who just discovered good sex."

"Only good?" he asks.

"I'm going to bed," I say on another yawn. "And I'm using the fourth bedroom on the right. I checked with Henry and Benedict and it's apparently free."

He raises his chin and narrows his gaze on me. Such expressive eyes. I can almost see all of the thoughts racing around inside his mind. But in the end, he says nothing. Which goes to prove that I am making the right choice by putting some space between us.

Because I can't have any privacy, Henry is sitting on the bed beside me wearing a designer suit when I wake. For a brief moment, I think it's Lucas. And the way my foolish heart is happy to have him close. To have him be the first thing I see. I need to have a stern talk with myself about making good choices. Especially when it comes to immortal men. No idea what nomad vampires are like, but the ones who congregate in families seem to be all about being in each other's company. But it makes sense that forever would get lonely sometimes.

As for me, I'm more used to being on my own. It's been over a decade since I left home for college and then settled in L.A. for work. Being in a big city can be lonely. Making friends as an adult can be hard. The gift of having a new family ready and willing to accept and support me through these wild times is beautiful. I still miss my human family. I'm not ashamed to say I cried myself to sleep again this morning. It hurts my dead heart to think of never seeing them again. Of never being a part of their lives. But I know Lucas is right, it's safer for me to keep my distance.

"Hey," I say. "What time is it?"

"The sun set almost an hour ago, sleepyhead," he says. "Happy fifth day as one of the undead. Father has already left for The Boulevard. He and Leilah had some things to discuss. We're to follow once you're ready. I put some outfit ideas on the chair over there, and I'll do your makeup and hair."

"Thanks."

"Did I ever tell you about the time I spent a couple of years touring the country with a theater company?" he asks. "It was 1910 and vaudeville was all the rage. There were singers, dancers, comedians, magicians, all sorts of acts really. We even crossed paths with Houdini once. Such an interesting fellow. It was a dreadful shame what happened to him. But back then, all we had to use for makeup was powder and lip stain and eyeshadow that came as a paste."

"That's where you learned how to do it?"

"I like to pick up skills here and there. It keeps things interesting. And makes me very popular with the ladies. Women love a man who knows how to be useful."

The bedroom I slept in has an opulent, cast-iron bed frame with cushions and blankets in various shades of blue. There's an empty armoire, a carved wooden Art Nouveau chair, and an en suite similar to Lucas's. Though, not as large. Nothing has been hung on the stone walls. I don't know if I slept any better in here. But my brain appreciates some distance from the object of my misguided and twisted affections. A chance to get my facts and thoughts straight. It was just good sex. It meant nothing. And I will keep telling myself as much until it becomes fact.

The painting of Ana is leaning against the stone wall.

"Why is that in here?" I ask, grabbing the waiting blood bag off the bedside table.

He gives me a sly smile. "Father said to take it down and ask you what you wanted done with it."

I keep on sipping the red stuff and try to hide my surprise.

"Should I start calling you Mother now, or wait for the official announcement? Mom. Mommy. No. Neither of those feel quite right. Mumsy, perhaps?"

"Shut up, Henry."

"I'm quite impressed with Father, really," he continues. "He doesn't have a fucking clue what he's doing with you. But bonus points for carrying on with confidence, regardless."

Wow, there is so much I am not going to say.

"Of course, he's had thousands of fuck buddies and such over the years. Despite being a lone wolf at heart, he has his needs. There have been a couple of times I thought he might actually be getting close to bonding with someone. But he inevitably always gave them a present and a pat on the butt and sent them on their way."

"You make him sound like an immortal fuckboy."

Henry laughs. "Please let me be there the first time you call him that to his face. I would take it as a personal favor."

"And how exactly is he a lone wolf when he has you and the rest of the family?"

"I meant romance-wise," he says. "Do try and keep up, sweetie. But to watch Father actually attempt to woo someone is...what's the word?"

"No idea."

Henry makes a humming noise. "Surprising. Absurd. Riotous. Something along those lines. Not that I don't support the idea wholeheartedly, don't get me wrong."

"I'm not even convinced that wooing me is what he's doing."

"No?"

"No," I confirm. "He killed me. Not that his brother didn't contribute to that situation."

"I'm not saying it's not complicated. But what relationship isn't?" Henry sighs. "I highly doubt he would bother jumping in front of a bullet for *me*. Not that I don't believe

I'm a loved and valued member of this family. But still...I think you make the old man feel things he hasn't experienced in a very long time."

"He gets off on bossing me around."

Henry snorts. "Did you seriously expect him to be a beta in the bedroom?"

"I don't know." If I frowned any harder my face would fall off. "I think you should mind your own business."

"Are you truly so against the idea of entering into a romantic relationship with Father? That's a pity."

"Henry—"

"Does him being a monster put you off? I understand the pulling out hearts and ripping off heads can be a lot." Henry gesticulates wildly. "But, sweetie, it's not like he does it for fun. Well. I mean, that's not to say he doesn't enjoy it occasionally. There was this one time in Bucharest... actually, I don't think he would appreciate me telling you that story. And you know even if he *finds* it fun, it's not like he actually *does* it for fun. You know, that doesn't sound so great, now that I say it out loud. But my point is, I do believe that he mostly only does the heart and head thing when necessary. *Mostly.*"

I stare at him in wonder.

"What?"

"Nothing," I say eventually. "And I understand that sort of thing is all tied up in vampire politics and so on."

"Exactly. What you need to remember is that he isn't human. He hasn't been for over a millennia. Your modern ways of thinking and how he sees the world are bound to clash upon occasion."

"I suppose so."

"Do you think Father incapable of maintaining such a relationship?"

I shake my head. "Honestly, I have no idea."

"Or perhaps you believe yourself to be unworthy of his attentions? He is, after all, rich, handsome, and powerful. I know plenty who would gnaw off a limb for a chance with him." He pauses and smiles. "Ha. That rhymed."

My mouth opens, but nothing comes out. *Shit*.

"That was also a trick question," says Henry, his voice rising in volume. "Little sister, how dare you put yourself down. I will not tolerate it!"

At which point, the bedroom door opens, and Benedict appears. His long blond hair is in a number of intricate braids, and he's wearing a navy suit with a matching tee beneath. "What are you yelling about?"

"I am outraged. Outraged, I tell you. She doesn't see that she is all things good and hot in this world."

I groan loud and proud.

"You do not see your beauty?" Benedict gazes at me in surprise. "Skye, I don't understand. The people of my village would have been greatly enamored of your bountiful breasts and childbearing hips."

Henry stares at him in abject horror.

"What?" asks Benedict.

"Oh my God, Vikings," says Henry. "You couldn't just say something nice about her hair or eyes or something?"

Benedict frowns. "I was trying to be honest."

"Wait," I say. "Why aren't you with Lucas?"

"Nicholas is with him," reports Benedict. "You are the known target at the moment and your safety is of importance to Lucas. A successful attack on you would also make the family appear weak."

"Right." I finish off the blood bag. "I better get ready so we can go."

"It should be interesting, if nothing else. They're having a big party to celebrate him joining the board and our takeover of The Boulevard," says Henry in his suit. "Father's exact words were, 'It is going to be a nice night with no drama where everyone gets along—or else.'"

Benedict grunts. "We'll see."

## ☾ CHAPTER TWELVE

Leilah's people stand security at the front doors of The Boulevard. A woman in business attire nods at us as we pass the reception desk. The hotel already seems different. Less dusty and decrepit. More alive despite many of the inhabitants being the undead.

Down in the subbasement level, the speakeasy is full to overflowing. A song by Billie Eilish pumps out of the sound system and waiters mingle carrying trays. There's a choice between a martini glass of blood or a flute of champagne. All of the glasses are crystal, of course—vampires love luxe. This is a party the likes of which I have never seen. All manner of clothing is on show. Top hat and tails, a kimono, a lace gown, and a sari.

A pair of amber eyes watch me from the back of the room. Neither human nor vampire.

Henry nods to a person wearing a tall white wig and a wide ornate dress. "He'll be wanting to hand out cake later. You know, one day Pierre will acknowledge that the French Revolution did, in fact, happen. This is the problem with many of our kind. They get stuck and time moves on without them."

Leilah holds court near the bar with Margaret at her side. And over by the door to the back room is a selection of green velvet couches. There sits Lucas. His gaze captures mine as soon as I'm in view, and all of the good and sensible reasons regarding why I should stay away go straight out the window. Not that there are any windows down here.

In an act of sheer bravery, and to give my self-doubt a kick in the pants, I wore the hottest dress on offer from Henry's selection. It is fire. A black gown with shoestring straps, a bodice that makes the most of my cleavage, and a full skirt with a split showing a lot of leg. My hair is in a sleek bun, and there's a pair of sky-high stiletto heels on my feet. I even broke out the diamond earrings he gave me for the evening.

When Lucas stands and holds out a hand to me, I can maybe admit I dressed up for a few reasons. To get this reaction from him, being one of them. To have him look at me like nothing else matters.

I was wrong. Sleeping in a different bedroom didn't change a thing. We seem to be on more of a collision course than ever. His grip is firm but gentle as he leads me to sit at his side. Not a word is spoken. There's this strange accord between us. He wants me with him and there's nowhere else I'd rather be. That's the truth of the matter.

He's wearing another of those perfectly fitted black suits with a matching button-down with his hair slicked back. It's a dark and dangerous sort of beauty. Nothing close to what I ever imagined for myself.

"So you are besotted with your newborn. If Samuel hadn't told me, I never would have believed it," says Rose, seated nearby with her husband. "Ripping off Archie's head makes sense to me now."

Samuel smiles knowingly and holds his mate's hand.

"He challenged me," says Lucas.

"Mm."

"You know how it is, Rose." Lucas passes me one of the martini glasses full of blood. "Skye here has been helping me adjust to this new century. That's all."

"Bullshit," she says in a voice not much above a whisper. "Your scent is all over her, and the way you watch her...I honestly didn't think you were capable of the finer feelings. But I understand why you would wish to downplay it. We'll talk of it no more."

I scowl. "It's not like I didn't shower."

Lucas doesn't respond. He, instead, turns to Henry and grimaces. "I asked you to dress presentably tonight."

"This is an Alexander McQueen graffiti suit, Father," says Henry. "I'm going to pretend you didn't say that."

Benedict joins Nicholas leaning against a wall nearby. Together they stand, talking quietly and watching the crowd. Nicholas is in black boots, pants, and a button-down with the sleeves rolled back. He doesn't bother to hide the pistol he wears in a shoulder holster. I am not ashamed to say I am wary of the man.

And all the while we're being watched. By vampires and humans and who knows what else. The weight of their gazes is a lot. I honestly don't know how Lucas and Rose tolerate it—being the focus of attention everywhere they go.

"Ming and Lucia were unable to attend," says Lucas. "But Javier dropped by earlier."

Henry nods. "Not surprising, given what's going on."

"What's going on?" I ask.

"A lot of vampires are entering the city. Some with connections to hostile families from other areas," says Samuel. "Trying to keep track of them all is next to impossible."

"You mean Lev's people?"

"Among others." Henry stares out at the crowd. "His sire was very unhappy at his failure to take L.A."

"He hasn't moved on from that yet?"

Rose smiles. "A few decades isn't so long for some."

"What happens next?" I ask, taking a sip of my drink.

"We wait," says Lucas. "There's been no further sign of my brother. But Nicholas will leave us soon to continue hunting. It's his job to flush him out."

I just nod.

"Who's the werewolf?" asks Henry.

Samuel runs his tongue over his teeth. "He's here representing several packs. Most notably from the mountains in the north and the desert to the west."

"Is that the owner of the amber eyes?" I ask. "That dude is huge."

"The wolves want to see how we handle things," says Lucas. "If Lev has let go of the idea of trying to take L.A., or if violence in the streets is about to escalate again."

"Would they get involved if it did?" I ask

"I don't know." Lucas rests his arm along the back of the couch. He soon frowns when he realizes he can't play with my hair because it's tied back in a bun. But he settles for toying with the zip on the back of my dress. Because of course, he does. "And I don't enjoy not knowing."

"I hate waiting," I say to no one in particular.

"It's the worst part of politics," agrees Samuel.

"You're a man of action." Rose plays with her ruby pendant. "But you know I reward your patience."

"That you do, my love."

"Oh, God," sighs Henry dramatically. "Is this what I have to look forward to? Watching Father and Skye be all cutesy and making kissy faces at each other for centuries?"

"Shut up, Henry," says Lucas without any heat.

"I heard a rumor that a faction of the wolves has expressed an interest in settling in the canyons," reports Samuel.

"Is that so?" asks Lucas.

All of a sudden, Henry's eyes widen, and he announces loudly, "Zofia, what a surprise!"

Nothing less than a goddess emerges from the crowd. Though, not an actual goddess. Long brown hair, white skin, pale blue eyes, and bone structure like a sculptor had a hand in her creation.

And Rose, Samuel, and Henry are suddenly behaving decidedly odd. Looking between me, Lucas, and the new arrival with a bit too much interest. I have such a bad feeling about all of this suddenly.

"Luca," says Zofia in a husky voice. "It's been a minute."

"Indeed, it has been. How are you?"

"I'd be just perfect if you'd dance with me?" Her smile is both sensual and inviting. Even I want to dance with her. Dammit.

"Of course." Lucas turns to me and says, "Back soon."

My answering smile is as weak as can be. But it doesn't matter, because he's already gone. He holds up a hand to signal to someone, and immediately the music is changed. They hold each other close and sway on the spot to a song by Ella Fitzgerald. The whispered conversation they have is interspersed with affectionate looks and ready smiles. It's obvious they know each other very well indeed.

I knew he had a history. And a long one at that. Guess I didn't quite consider what it would be like to come face to face with the same. Zofia appears to be about a decade older than me, gorgeous and graceful. Anyone would forgive me for having a moment. He did, however, say he'd be back soon.

"Zofia and Lucas are old friends," explains Rose with a sympathetic expression.

Henry, however, is not happy. "The truth, little sister, is that they were fuckbuddies from around the time we arrived in California to when Father decided to take his nap. Not quite a century."

"Huh. That's a long time." My smile is small. "And to think he told me he was a virgin. I can't believe he'd lie to me about something like that."

Samuel's laughter is soft and low. "Skye, did I ever tell you about the first time I took my lovely wife here out on a date? There I am, trying desperately to impress her, and we run into her ex. No less than a crown prince destined for the throne."

"Only of a very small country. It hardly mattered at all." Rose winks at me.

"I asked her why she didn't want to be a queen, and she told me..."

Rose's gaze is full of warmth. "Crowns are uncomfortable as fuck."

"That's true, actually." Henry smiles despite himself. "Father has collected a couple over the years. A tiara isn't too bad; though, they can pinch. But a full-on, gold-and-gemstone-laden crown...ugh. Such a headache, and the strain it puts on one's neck."

"I'm sure you looked stunning just the same."

"Thank you, Rose. I did." Henry turns back to watch the only couple dancing in the club. "Last I heard, Zofia had settled in Poland. I wonder what she's doing here."

Samuel shakes his head. "I don't know."

Henry gives me a long look. "Try not to worry, sweetie. Father might be a monster, but he is not a cheater."

"We don't have that sort of relationship, Henry."

He doesn't bother to reply.

"How are you all doing over here?" asks Leilah, sweeping in and sitting by my side. She watches Lucas and Zofia dancing for a minute. Then gives me a reassuring smile.

"Appease my curiosity, Leilah," says Rose. "Why haven't you broken off and become head of your own family?"

"Why spend my own money when I can use the old man's?"

Henry laughs.

"This place, for instance." She waves her hand at the room. "It will take many millions to renovate it to my exacting standards. And while Lucas will be paying the bill, I'll be the one in charge and reaping much of the rewards. Of course, I share this information with you so honestly and openly because not only are you a dear friend to our family, but doubtless your mate has already been whispering in your ear about it."

Rose's smile is coy. "He whispers in my ear about a good many things."

I swear Samuel blushes.

"If the old man ever cut the purse strings or we began to disagree, then we might have a problem," says Leilah.

"That's never going to happen." Henry shakes his head. "You're the only one of his children inclined to sire more vampires and train them to be useful. It's why he made you heir."

"Mm." Leilah flips her hair back over one shoulder. The woman is the epitome of glamor. Her being heir is news to me. She seems a smart choice, however. "It's good to have company, little brother. One day you might find a human you would prefer not to live without."

"Doubtful," says Henry.

The way I resist the urge to watch Lucas with all my might...someone should give me a medal. Or at least a cookie.

"Are you expecting a rush on turning newborns now that the rules are lifted?" asks Henry.

"That's happened?" I ask in surprise.

Rose nods. "I don't necessarily believe there'll be a rush. Most of our kind have seen how much easier and less complicated life is with fewer of us around. But we'll see. Reactions to us decreasing the patrolling of the city is a bigger concern."

"It pays to be cautious, and the creatures in L.A. know that. No one wants another cull." Henry sighs. "Is it true two bodies were found drained of blood and left in public spaces this morning?"

Samuel's lips thin in irritation. "Yes. Long Beach and Pasadena."

"Hopefully just a few foolish vampires acting out," says Rose. "They're being hunted as we speak. But I understand some of the parties celebrating the easing of the rules were quite rowdy."

"We'll find them. Sooner or later."

Henry throws a leg over the arm of the chair and says nothing.

I take another sip of blood. Not sure where they get the good stuff from, but it tastes so much better than my usual fare from plastic bags. "This world is so complicated."

"Feeling overwhelmed?" asks Leilah. "Give yourself time. It's a lot to adjust to."

And Lucas and Zofia dance on. She throws her head back and laughs and ugh. I can't do this. Not with all of these people watching me from the crowd. Having all of these emotions about him in the first place is discombobulating as fuck. I rise from my seat with my clutch in hand and say, "Back in a moment."

"Where are you going," asks Henry, who has already jumped to his feet.

"Just to check my makeup."

"I did your makeup. It's flawless. What are you insinuating?"

I think calm thoughts and smile. "Henry, be calm. I just need a moment."

"All of these nosy assholes watching all the time," says Leilah. "I don't blame you for wanting a break. Lucas and the Woodsman legend was bad enough before he went into hiding for seventy years. Now it's out of control."

Henry grunts. "You're not going to hide away and cry, are you? Father doesn't like it when you cry. But he especially doesn't like you crying on your own."

"No, I'm not going to cry," I say.

Henry just gives me a look. I have no idea what it means.

"Human girls go to bathrooms in groups, I'm told," says Leilah. "Would you like some company?"

"I'm fine. But thank you."

She nods and searches the crowd for Margaret. Her partner stands at the bar with a glass of scotch or similar in her hand. And the look they share...I want that. The open affection and support they show each other. To go through life together as they do. It's a beautiful idea. Though, I don't know how practical it is, since my current crush is dancing with his ex-hookup who looks like a supermodel.

Eh. Whatever. As my mother once told me, you can't control what other people do, you can only control how you react to same.

"I'll walk you to the door," says Henry, in an unusually no-nonsense tone.

Benedict watches us go. Nicholas seems to have disappeared. Guess he's gone hunting.

In a dark hallway off to the side is the bathroom. A pack of giggling humans stumble out and hurry past me. Though, one bares his neck in what I assume is a tease. He should really be more careful. My control is getting better each night. But it's still not great. The familiar sound of their blood rushing through their veins, the warmth of their bodies, and the scent of them is all right there, making my mouth water.

Henry snaps his teeth playfully at the group. I hustle my ass into the bathroom and ignore them as best I can. To think that less than a week ago, I was one of them. A real live mortal girl with a beating heart and working lungs and all the rest. Now I am this magical, messed-up thing. Who knew being undead came with such a complicated romantic life?

Henry was right, my makeup is flawless. I touch up my nude lipstick just the same. The music from the bar is reduced to a muted thump in here. Whoever built this place put in some seriously thick walls. To have no one near me waiting or watching for a moment is exactly what I wanted. I stretch my neck and roll my shoulders. Just generally trying to decompress. Sometimes you need some space and silence. Along with the administration of a healthy dose of self-respect.

The woman in the mirror is fire. I've never looked so good in my life. And if Lucas doesn't appreciate that fact, then he can go fuck himself. Honestly.

A loud thud comes from out in the hallway, making me jump. It almost sounds like some sort of skirmish is taking place. Then I hear a faint scraping noise behind me, someone moving or something. But it's too late to so much as turn because the whole world goes dark.

## ☾ CHAPTER THIRTEEN

The hard smack of an open palm hitting me on the cheek wakes me up. I gasp and jerk back to evade more of the same, but there's nothing I can do. Nowhere I can go. I am slumped uncomfortably on the floor. My hands are secured behind my back to a steel post, and silver chains are burning my skin. My face stings, though the pain soon fades. I don't think I've ever actually been hit before—at least not in the face like this.

The last thing I remember is being in the bathroom and hearing the noise from behind me. My shoes and clutch are missing. And the back of my head hurts. Guess they knocked me out to bring me here. Though, if they did, I would have thought an injury like that would be healed by now. But I feel dizzy and weak, and I don't know what.

This is bad. Really bad. It looks like I'm in another basement. This one, however, lacks all of the faded charm of the speakeasy. Concrete walls, three thugs, and a selection of implements just perfect for torture laid out on the floor. A hammer, pliers, a saw, some knives, and a baseball bat. Along with scissors, a steak knife, a jar of salt, and needle and thread. No idea what the last few things would be used for. But none of it is giving me comfort.

Two of the thugs are vampires, but one is human. I can hear his galloping heart inside his chest. Somebody else besides me is nervous.

I lived the whole of my mortal life without being of much interest to anyone. To now be the subject of all this attention is both bizarre and awful.

"She's awake," mumbles one of them. "Are you sure you got all of the bugs off her clothing? Last fucking thing we need is the Woodsman tracking her here."

Tracking devices in my clothing and accessories sounds about right. Very Lucas. The assholes finding them is not good. What I need to do is stay calm and think. But I have the distinct feeling I'm on the verge of the biggest panic attack of my life. Or death. I might also just slide back into unconsciousness. Black spots are dancing before my eyes.

Someone must have noticed me missing by now. The family will be looking for me. I'd love to know how they got me out of The Boulevard. In all likelihood through another of those hidden passageways Nicholas was talking about. Not to be harsh, but I officially kind of hate that hotel.

Lucas will find me. I know he will. I just don't know if he'll find me while I'm still in one piece. Therefore, I am going to have to help myself.

"I'll take those," says another of the thugs, getting in my face. I focus on him, concentrating hard, searching for the still part of my mind, and it actually works. The word that appears inside my head is *bored*. Abduction and assault have lost their thrill for him, apparently. But the emotion accompanying the word is greed. Which makes perfect sense when he kneels in front of me and rips out my diamond earrings. Just tears the hooks through the flesh of my earlobes.

My howls of pain fill the room. A few drops of blood fall onto my bare shoulders. I have no tolerance for pain. Never have. Therefore, being tortured is a problem for me. A really fucking big one.

"Stupid bitch," mutters the second vampire, and he kicks me in the thigh with his steel-toed boots. Once, twice, three times, making me scream in pain even louder. He doesn't stop until the sound of cracking echoes in the cold, empty space. My upper leg is a mass of bruises ever so slowly changing color by the barest of degrees. I am not healing anywhere near as fast as I should. And he just broke the thickest damn bone in my body with relative ease. Shit.

At this point, I burst into tears. I can't help it. Fear owns me completely. I have never been so scared in my life. Not even when Lucas turned me, which is saying something. Speaking of my sire, I would dearly love to know where he is right now.

All three of the assholes start laughing at me. Guess I make a pretty pathetic figure, sitting on the ground, sobbing. My leg is sheer agony. I am helpless, and I hate it.

"Let's get a drink," says one vampire to the other. Then he turns to the human. "Watch her."

"What?" asks the human in a high-pitched voice. "You're leaving me on my own?"

"It's not like she's going anywhere with a broken femur," the second vampire scoffs. "That's why we bled her, you idiot. So she wouldn't have the strength to heal herself. And she's too new to be able to compel you. That shit takes years to learn."

The human frowns his whole heart out. "Yeah, but—"

"You're not actually scared of this pitiful, bawling newborn, are you? All you have to do is stand here and keep an eye on her. Just don't get too close. You'll be fine."

"He'll be here soon," says the first vampire. And a word appears inside my head, surrounded by a wary sort of respect. *Marc.* Which makes perfect sense.

Then the two vampires walk out, shutting the door behind them. The way it echoes hollowly is like something out of a horror film.

I huddle on the floor, sniffling. The pain in my leg is easing ever so slowly as the bone knits itself back together. Thank goodness. But fuck, it hurts. Having a bone broken and feeling it heal just might be the most excruciating thing ever.

It is not, however, unusual for me to be underestimated. In work environments, by boyfriends, etcetera. And this situation is no different. If they think I'm going to sit here docilely waiting to get tortured, they are kidding themselves. I refuse to end like this. These assholes will not be what kills me. Not when me being undead was starting to show such promise.

"Please don't hurt me," I whisper, watching him through my lashes.

"Shut up," he says, staring off at the wall.

"I can turn you. That's what you want, isn't it? That's why you're with them?"

The human pulls a gun no doubt loaded with wooden bullets out of the back of his pants. His brows draw tight together as he frowns.

"Don't you want to be immortal and live forever?"

"You were only just turned. You probably can't even do that yet."

"But I was turned by the Woodsman. His blood is stronger than his brother's. You know that, right?"

He shrugs and scowls at the ground. But he's listening. I have his attention.

"And I'm his favorite," I say with a forced smile. I really should have been practicing this mind control stuff before now. More than just the one time with Henry. But I push as hard as I can, forcing my focus onto him, all while searching again for the still and silent part of my mind. The place where other people's words and feelings seem to appear to me out of nowhere. This has to work. It just has to. "He gave me those diamond earrings. Help me, and he'll give you even more. He's got cars and jewels and whatever you want."

"Look, would you just..."

And I have him. It actually works! The muscles in his face slacken and his gaze goes dazed. That's the thing with humans...they're trained from a young age to look at people when speaking to them. Hooray for having good manners.

"Get the chains off me," I say. "Now."

He rushes to do my bidding, dropping the gun on the floor in the process. A couple of layers of my skin peel away with the silver chains, which stings like hell. But at least I'm free. My leg doesn't want to support me at first. A break obviously takes a while to heal. I, however, don't have time to waste. The great thing about a background in administration is the ability to give clear and concise instructions under pressure.

"Pick up your gun and go shoot the vampires outside," I order. "Be quick. Use all your bullets. Aim to kill."

He all but runs for the door with his weapon back in hand. I limp over to the selection of torture implements. I'm going to need all the help I can get. The long, sharp, serrated knife is tempting. Same goes for the hammer. But in the end, I grab the old baseball bat with a selection of truly dubious dark stains in the wood. Keeping some distance between me and them seems smart. Not having to get in quite so close to cause the most damage is paramount.

I swing it a time or two to test my arm. It's about time my childhood P.E. classes come in handy for something.

The bang of the gun goes off again and again outside.

Time to go. If Marc catches me here, it will not be fun. A broken femur will be the least of my worries.

Outside are a lot of pipes and electrical wiring with the same concrete walls. We're in a basement underneath a big building, but that's about all I can tell. This time the concrete rooms form masses of hallways running every which way. Some random human stands there screaming. It's a shrill, piercing sort of sound. Blood seeps from the messy bite wound on his neck. The way the scent of it calls to me, making my mouth water, gives me pause.

One of the vampires is already on the ground with a gunshot wound smack bam center of the forehead. His body turns to ash before my eyes. Seems my hypnotized human knows his way around a gun. Lucky me. But the other one is fighting back despite a nasty bullet graze across his face and one embedded in his chest.

My hypnotized human fires the remainder of his bullets. Another hits center body mass before the gun clicks empty. However, the vampire is still standing. Not okay. I am done with being hurt today, so this asshole has got to die.

Right now, while he's focusing on the human instead of me. Because the element of surprise is my very best friend.

Without hesitation, I rush him and swing. The meaty thwack of the bat hitting the side of his head is disgusting. Just truly fucking awful. How his skull caves in and everything. Down he goes, lying still at my feet. I bare my teeth and bring the bat down on his head two more times. Then he finally turns to ash.

To the screaming human, I say, "Be quiet and follow us." Then I turn to my friend with the gun and order, "Show me the fastest and safest way out of here."

The human leads us through a maze of tunnels. With each step my leg is a little stronger, but it's still not great. My bare feet scrape against the cold, dirty ground. When we reach an elevator, my stomach twists nervously. Here is where the people always get caught in the movies. When they're almost out and safe. It's when the bad guy arrives, and everything goes to Hell.

But the elevator dings and the doors slide open and it's empty. I could almost cry again from relief.

As soon as we're inside, I drop the bat and grab the guy with the gun. I need what he has. I have to heal. As soon as I sink my teeth into his neck, fresh warm blood fills my mouth. It tastes so damn good. Much better than the packaged stuff. Lucas was right about that. It rushes through me, strengthening me.

I drink and drink, and it doesn't even occur to me not to drain him of every last drop. Nothing could stop me from taking it all. Which is horrifying, but I don't have time to deal with the morality of it right now. His heartbeat slows before it finally stops. I toss his body into the corner. Hard to feel bad about killing someone who was more than willing to do the same to me.

The other human stands docile and silent. But the look in his eyes says I'm a monster. And he's right. He is absolutely right. Because I just killed someone without hesitation, and I am absolutely willing to do it again to get out of here.

With the fresh blood in me, I feel a lot better. Ignoring the twinges and lingering ache in my leg, I pick up the bat and hold it in a good tight grip. Ready for whatever awaits us. The sire bond thing in my chest tugs...Lucas is reaching out to me. But it's not like I can answer him. I don't even know if he has a phone number for the house. Nor do I have any money or anything useful on me.

We arrive at the ground floor and the doors slide open. It's a pretty standard sort of lobby. Rows of mailboxes and a plastic potted plant. Along with another vampire guard. His head rolls across the floor as his body crumples. Then both turn to ash.

And standing there with an axe in hand is Lucas.

I have never been happier to see someone in my life. Seems my undead heart is every bit as messy as my beating one was. Because the need I have to throw myself into his arms and cry up a storm is huge. But I guess I am becoming more vampire minded, because the idea of looking weak grates at me.

"Hello, little sister," says Henry, standing behind him. Blood covers the front of his white button-down shirt. "We've been looking for you. So rude to leave a party without saying goodbye. I, for one, was outraged at such shoddy behavior."

"I think we can safely assume it wasn't by choice." Lucas's gaze is frantic while his lips are a straight, pissed-off line. "Look at me. Are you okay?"

I nod. "Yeah."

The tension in his shoulders eases just a little at my words. But he still doesn't seem happy.

"Henry, what happened to you?"

"There I was, waiting for you in the hallway, when some idiot tried to stake me. Can you believe that shit?" he asks, with comically wide eyes. "Sadly for them, they botched the job and wound up on the receiving end of that particular piece of sharpened wood."

"Thank goodness for that."

"I found the entrance they used hidden in a wall. But you were already gone. I am sorry for failing you."

I attempt a smile. "Getting kidnapped from a bathroom wasn't on either of our bingo cards."

Henry just sighs.

Benedict gives me a wink. "Nice baseball bat."

"Very Father coded, isn't it?" asks Henry. "I told you they make a nice couple."

I turn back and tell the remaining human, "Run. Get to safety."

"Skye, you're limping and there's blood on you. Let me try another question, and hopefully this time you'll give me an honest response," says Lucas. "Who hurt you?"

"Thugs hired by Marc."

Lucas growls low in his throat. "I am going to fucking kill them. Then, for once and for all, I am going to kill my brother."

"You can't."

"Oh yes, I can."

"No," I say patiently. "You can't kill them because I already did that. But feel free to put an end to your brother. I would really appreciate it."

There's no imagining the surprise on their faces. Lucas just blinks. "You killed them?"

"Yes. I mean...I had some help, but...yeah."

"Huh," says Henry. "Good job, little sister."

Nicholas gives me a nod of approval.

With the fresh blood in me, I can move more easily. My hair is half in, half out of the now-lopsided bun, and my evening dress is bedraggled. No idea what my makeup is like; though, I doubt it's good with the amount of crying I've been doing. Just about every nail is chipped or broken. It shouldn't matter that I'm a wreck. But everything seems to be catching up with me now.

Lucas holds out a hand and I reach for it, but my own is streaked with blood and ash. Just covered in it. And I don't like the way my limb is shaking either.

The sky outside is lightening. I can feel it care of the lethargy creeping into my limbs. It's like the dawn has this deadly pull on me. An entire night was lost to this kidnapping fuckery. What a waste.

"It's decision time. We staying or going?" asks Nico.

I frown. "But Marc—"

"Isn't here," says Lucas. "He was just sighted to the north of the city. Samuel informed us a few minutes ago."

"He's not here?"

Lucas shakes his head. "You need to feed and rest. And we need to discuss next steps. Do you need me to carry you?"

"No," I say. "Thank you."

Outside is Benedict's G Wagon for us and a Ducati motorbike for Nico. Lucas hovers as I limp along. We're not even that far from home or the hotel. Marc's goons obviously didn't hide me all that well. Not knowing I have secret psychic powers giving me a kick along in this life is one thing. But their general ineptness is a little bewildering. Leaving me alone with the human whom I might have managed to overpower, etcetera. I don't know. It just doesn't quite make sense. Tonight is probably a prime example of getting what you paid for because Marc's goons were not great at their jobs.

I wince when I put my weight on my leg climbing out of the vehicle at home. But it's almost back to normal. Three stories of white walls and terracotta roof tiles tower over me. It's never been a more welcome sight. The scent of the climbing roses and jasmine. I made it back in one piece. Go me.

Nico escorts us home, then rides off at speed. Hunting our enemies, no doubt.

Lucas sweeps me up into his arms. "Enough."

"I can walk."

"Not well, you can't."

I loop my arms around his neck as we head down to the basement lair. He says nothing as he carries me through his bedroom and into his en suite. There, he carefully sets me down so he can start running a bath. Steam starts to billow as hot water slowly fills the tub.

He grabs a face towel and wets it before taking my chin in hand. "Let's get the dried blood off your face."

"I fed on someone and killed them. The human they had with them."

"You did what you had to." He tosses the dirty towel into the sink and drops to his knees to examine my leg. Strong hands gently feel along the line of the bone leading up to my hip. The man does not look happy; though, he says, "It seems to be healing satisfactorily."

"Yeah."

He stands and toes off his shoes. "Tell me everything that happened in as much detail as possible. Don't leave anything out."

And I do as told. His getting naked, however, is damn distracting. It works to break through the shock. My brain seems to be doing better at dealing with the here and now. At calming down and feeling safe in this moment.

By the time I'm finished talking, he's down to nothing. Even at his ease, he's a sight to behold. Not that I stare at his crotch or anything because that would be awkward. While I'm not sure exactly what we're doing, I don't think this is about sex. He doesn't seem to be giving off those vibes right now. Which is a good thing. The events of tonight have left me feeling fragile.

"Stand up," he says, then he undoes the zipper on the back of my dress. My strapless bra and panties are soon gone, too. He climbs into the bath, then holds out a hand to me. It is nice to know I'm not alone. I think I need some company right now.

I sit between his legs, my back to his front. The hot water is heavenly. Having the solid strength of his body pressed against me is even better. I am home and safe and everything is okay. For the moment, at least.

First thing, I wash all of the makeup off my face. Lucas starts pulling the pins out of my messy hair and dropping them on the floor. Not stopping until my hair hangs loose. Then he combs it with his fingers, working out the worst of the tangles with more patience than I would have given him credit for.

"You really killed two vampires and a human?" he asks with an edge of surprise.

"Yeah. Basically. I did things tonight I never imagined I would have to do, and it was...I don't know. I try to be a kind person. Mostly," I say. "But the rules change when someone wants to torture and kill you. I don't know how else to explain it. Guess we're both monsters now."

He grunts.

"That's all you've got to say?"

He sighs. "Skye, why did you want to go off on your own at the hotel?"

"I just needed a moment. You're used to these things, with everyone staring at you. They still weird me out."

"You weren't jealous of Zofia?"

To be honest, I had forgotten all about her. I rest my head back against his shoulder and think it over. "A little, maybe. But not really."

"Please explain."

"We banged once on your office desk," I say. "It doesn't equate to a situation where I believe I have any rights over you."

"Mm."

"Zofia is very beautiful. I might have liked to dance with her myself."

He goes from lazily tracing a finger back and forth along the length of my arm, to having his hand wrapped firmly around my throat in an instant. "No, Skye."

"Speaking of jealousy."

"The difference between us is...I am not pretending otherwise."

I don't know what to say to that.

He presses a kiss to my forehead and, a finger at a time, releases the hold on my throat. I don't know if it's all vampires, or just this one in particular. But they are emotional quicksand. I never know where I'm standing, let alone how fast I'm sinking.

"We haven't even known each other a full week," I say in a quiet voice.

"What's that got to do with it?"

"Well..."

"Do you think after fifteen-hundred years, I don't know my own mind?" he asks in his usual calm tone. "I assure you, I do."

"That's not what I meant."

"And what I want is *you*, so I am going to have you."

I wrinkle my nose. "What about what I want?"

"Your wants and needs are important and will be seen to. By me."

"No." I shake my head. "Lucas, we're not—"

"Yes, Skye, we are."

And with that, he rises and steps out of the bath, reaching for a towel. Watching the water running off his body might have me inspired to write bad poetry. It is definitely harder to be angry at him when he's naked. Not to be shallow or anything. But the magnificence of his buttocks really shouldn't be underestimated.

"I have some things to discuss with the others," he says. "I trust you're fine on your own?"

"This conversation isn't over."

He doesn't even bother to answer. Just walks through to his bedroom, toweling off his dark hair.

*What the hell have I gotten myself into?*

## ☾ CHAPTER FOURTEEN

I wake up screaming, sitting bolt upright on the white, cast-iron bed. A moment later the door crashes open and Lucas is there. He grips my shoulders and studies my tear-stained face. My mind is a mess. The remnants of the nightmare are fading, leaving confusion and fear.

"Skye," he says in a firm voice. "Look at me. Are you all right?"

"Yes. Yeah, I...shit." I put a hand to his chest and push. He sits back on the mattress, giving me space while I wipe my cheeks dry. Only the dim light from the candles in the parlor light the room. Everything is shadows. "It was just a nightmare."

He nods.

"I didn't even think vampires had nightmares or dreams."

"The mind is a complex thing, sweetie," says Henry from the doorway. "Trauma can mess with you in all sorts of ways. But you're safe here with us."

"Or maybe you don't feel as secure in this room on your own. That's easily fixed." Lucas lifts me and the blanket off the bed. The way he picks me up as if I weigh nothing and carries me around so carefully like I am precious. I kind of need it right now.

"You get that you're a bully, right?" I ask as he carries me down the hallway back to his bedroom. "I mean, you've made peace with that aspect of your personality."

"Oh, yes," says Henry, tailing along behind us. "That's old news. Did I ever tell you about the time in Natal when he—"

And that's when Lucas kicks the bedroom door shut in his face.

"Harsh," shouts Henry from out in the hallway.

Lucas sets me on the bed with one of his trademark frowns. He's wearing a black tee, jeans, and boots. The modern look sure does suit him. Though, he's so pretty he could pull off anything. I'm in another expensive sleep set made of linen. A flickering white pillar candle sits on the desk. He might have a point; I do like his room. The chunky, wooden four-poster bed and the scent of his cologne lingering in the air. The pictures and so on. How the décor offers hints of his existence through the ages.

"Do you want to tell me about your dream?" he asks.

"No." I shake my head. "Better to just forget it. What time is it?"

"It's almost sunset," he says. "But you should try to go back to sleep. I'll watch over you."

"Keep me safe from the demons in my head?" I play with a loose thread on the blanket. And wind up accidentally tearing the thick, woolen material. Just when I thought I had my strength under control. The way that clumsiness remains my chosen undead aesthetic.

He just sits there staring at me all the while. There's such intensity in his gaze. Like he can read me inside and out; all of my hopes and dreams open to him for perusal. No one has ever been this interested in me. I'm going to miss it when it goes. When his attention moves on to other topics.

"You shouldn't look at me that way," I say.

"How should I look at you?"

It's a good question. One I can't answer. Or maybe I don't want to answer. I give my ponytail a nervous tug. "I was jealous about your ex."

"I know."

The ego on this guy. I shoot him a dirty look, which of course, achieves nothing. "The human whom I fed from...in my dream, I tore him apart to get at the blood."

"It's certainly one way to do it; though, there are less messier choices," he says in his usual dry tone. "Ones less inclined toward waste."

"You're such an ass."

The edge of his mouth rises in a smirk.

I square my shoulders and take a deep, unnecessary breath. Habits really do die hard. "I need to know if you're going to be yet another one of those people who like the idea they have of me, but then when they get to know me, they're disappointed."

He narrows his gaze on me. Then he stands and walks over to the desk. Among the books and so on sits a blue silk case. This, along with a large white envelope, are what he returns with. He gives me the case first. "Open it, Skye."

Inside are a pair of diamond drop earrings and a matching necklace with stars. The stones range in size from small to astonishing. It must be worth millions. I don't know what to say.

"To replace the jewelry that was stolen from you," he says. Then he gives me the envelope. "These are the documents Helena sent over. They detail your settlement from The Thorn Group."

"You opened my mail?"

"That's beside the point. Note the payout you're receiving."

I skim the document and wow. There are, indeed, a lot of zeros. "Wow."

"I was born in a time when women were considered the property of men."

"Some idiots still think that way today."

He nods. "I won't lie to you, it's an attractive idea. I would like to own you. But you're not the type to thrive in such a relationship. You would find it claustrophobic and limiting. Nor do I necessarily require such control."

The way I hold in any and all sarcastic comments. I deserve an award. I am also dying to know where he's heading with this.

"You have money. And you've made friends, vampires who would offer you their protection and assistance. For instance, Leilah is willing to let you join her at the hotel. She would ensure you were not removed from the premises against your will again."

"Is that so?"

"Yes. You should know Lev has gone north for now. Nicholas is tracking him digitally through cameras and such. His human servants are moving him during the daylight hours. We believe his maker summoned him. No doubt he'll eventually return, but the danger to you from that region is not as immediate."

"What about your brother?"

His gaze blanks. "The hunt begins as soon as the sun sets. I will find him and kill him."

"What are you saying with all of this?"

"That strictly speaking, you no longer need me." He pauses. "And should you choose to leave, I would do my utmost to respect that choice."

I don't know why I'm smiling. "You would do your utmost?"

"Yes," he says. "Benedict explained that modern women must have choices. That their rights must be equal."

"Benedict explained all of that?"

He nods. "It would be difficult for me. But I've given it some thought. I believe if I stayed close to you and was able to watch over you, that would fulfill this need in me. For a time, at least."

"Did you actually just admit to planning to stalk me?"

He lifts one shoulder in an elegant shrug. "The way I am with you is strange and new to me. I cannot explain it, but denying it is pointless."

"So, what you're basically saying is that I can leave you, but you're coming, too."

He thinks it over and nods. "That about sums it up."

"Lucas—"

"You should get some sleep. Even Henry has been resting today, and he has centuries on you. Healing takes energy."

He has a point. But my mind is busy as fuck. "I keep thinking about the instruments of torture they had lined up waiting for me in that place. The knives and hammer and saw are all pretty obvious. But what were they going to do with the salt and the needle and thread?"

"Salt in a wound hurts and it delays healing."

"Oh."

"As for the needle and thread...I am not sure."

"I watched a show once where they sewed a person's lips shut as some sort of strange punishment." And just the thought of such a thing sends a shiver down my spine. "So gross."

"Most anything is believable of my brother. Though, I've never heard of Marc doing such a thing."

"I want you to use me as bait to lure him out," I say before my courage can desert me.

"What?" snaps Lucas. "No. Absolutely not."

"We need this to end. I refuse to spend every night looking over my shoulder. Just waiting for him to mess with me some more."

"Skye, he will be found and dealt with. I promise you."

"I don't want anyone else being sent back as ashes in a box, either."

His lips flatline.

"Using me makes sense. You know it does. We can turn his weird fixation with me into a positive. Lure him into a trap and finish him once and for all."

"You're not going to let this go, are you?"

"No," I say. "I'm not. You said this was a family, and I am supposed to be part of it. So let me help solve this problem."

His sigh is mighty. "I will consider your offer. But first you will allow Nico and me to track him and attempt to deal with him our way."

I just nod. It's the best response I'm going to get for now. "The needle and thread were fine."

"What?"

"The needle and thread with the torture stuff. They weren't thick. Wouldn't you need something substantial to push through skin?"

Lucas just looks at me, saying nothing for a long moment, and then, "Skye, what color was the thread?"

"Black."

"Like your dress."

"Yes."

And he's gone. It takes me a moment longer to follow him into the bathroom, where my abandoned dress is laying on the ground. Lucas inspects the seams of the garment, and then the hem.

"What are you looking for?" I ask.

"Not sure. But I'll know it when I find it."

"They left one human to guard me," I say, thinking aloud. "I know I'm only a newborn. But it still seemed weird. Then there's how fast you found me, and the fact that Marc wasn't even in the vicinity."

"Nico tracked the vehicle they used. Security cameras at The Boulevard and CCTV made the process quite quick and easy."

"That's my point."

Lucas pauses and carefully proceeds to unpick a segment of thread. Some stitching that's not as neat and perfect as the rest around the bottom of the skirt. From within the section, a silver medallion falls onto the ground. There's some sort of symbol carved into it. With words curling around and around on the other side. I've always had a good imagination, but there's no way I am imagining the bad vibes emanating from the thing. Now that it's out in the open, it's like ill will flows freely from the medal.

"What is it?" I ask, leaning in to try and read it. However, the writing is in no language I've ever seen. "Lucas?"

"Powerful magic intended to counteract the runes and allow our enemies to enter. My brother and his Russian friends must have paid a pretty penny for it."

The pieces fall into place in my mind and my lip curls in a very vampire-style snarl. "That's why they kidnapped me...so they could plant that thing on me and have me walk it right on into the house for them."

He raises his head, and I feel the tug in the middle of my chest. It's the sire bond being used—and not just on me. As evidenced when Henry and Benedict stride into the room. "Get ready," says Lucas. "We're about to have guests."

Not even Marc is willing to fuck with the sun. Or not too much. When the attack begins, our nearest star has just met the horizon. I can feel it still warning me to keep my head down, to stay hidden or else. It would take a strong will to ignore it. Either that, or a burning hatred nurtured over a thousand or so years and a shitload of money.

Marc must have hired humans to transport him and his people here and bring them inside out of the daylight. Several large vehicles park in the drive. Some sort of vans or trucks or something. I get the feeling we're about to be seriously outnumbered. Car doors open and close. But there's no murmur of conversation. Not a single word is said, only footsteps and the sound of heavy boxes being brought inside the house. With the runes negated, there's nothing to keep them out.

Had we not found the medallion, they probably would have taken us by surprise. I would, in all likelihood, have been asleep and not heard *slaughter* and *deception* in the still and silent corner of my mind. Missed the heightened emotions surrounding these words. All of the anticipation and anger.

The others might well have thought they were just from The Thorn Group. Contractors hired to see to the house or garden. Such workers have been coming and going during the daylight hours. There have also been deliveries. So many deliveries. Items Lucas has asked for or Shirley collected for him over the years. It's late in the day for humans to be here. But certainly not beyond the realm of possibility.

Lucas decided not to destroy the medallion or throw it out the nearest window. This is his chance to finally face his brother on home ground. He wanted me to hide in a tunnel, one of the secret other exits, until it was over. But they're going to need every hand they can get. Even a shaky one with little to no experience. Nicholas and Leilah will be here as soon as the sun is fully set. But I have the distinct feeling they're going to be too late.

My anxiety is as high as can be, despite our home seeming so normal. Pillar candles burn in the lounge room belowground, and a record is playing. Billie Holiday sings oh so sweetly. The heavy wooden door at the back of the basement stands open a hand's width. It's a welcoming scene, typical of how the days are spent by family members who don't need to sleep. Ones who believe themselves safe, care of the runes.

Lucas and I stand to the side of the back hallway. As close as he would let me get to the action. But I can see everything and have a pistol in hand. Something I have agreed only to use as a last resort. None of the family is keen to experience friendly fire. Which, to be fair, could very well happen. However, there's no way I was willing to agree to being unarmed when we're under attack.

Then suddenly it begins. I didn't even hear anyone approach the door. These people are seriously good.

The door opens wider, slowly and silently. And the first of Marc's assassins steps inside with a submachine gun. He sprays the room with wooden bullets, making crystal and porcelain shatter as feathers and fluff from the furniture fills the air. It's a fucking mess.

Benedict rises from behind the chaise and a dagger flies from his hand. Of course, the point finds its target, burying itself deep in the creature's eye. The vampire turns to ash where he stands.

Another immediately steps forward to take his place. This time it's a petite woman wielding her own sharp implements. As evidenced by the throwing star now sticking out of Benedict's shoulder. But Henry rises from behind an antique credenza with a pistol in hand. One, two, three bullets hit her heart, and she, too, is ash.

It all happens so quickly. To each action, an equally bloody and violent reaction.

One at a time doesn't seem to be working for them. Or perhaps Marc runs out of patience. Because five vampires rush the room. The first falling at shots from Henry. And the second suddenly has a spear sticking out of his chest. Benedict surges forward with a short sword in hand. He removes a creature's head from its body with relative ease. But a bullet from another hits Benedict, and he snarls in pain.

Henry drops his pistol and draws a pair of daggers from the leather harness he wears on his chest. It's like a brutal dance, seeing him and an enemy circle each other. Then knives flash and Henry grunts as a long streak of blood appears on his back. Ouch.

His enemy grins, beyond pleased. They start moving so fast it's hard to track. Meanwhile, another falls to Benedict's sword. He strikes and parries with ease, dealing out death with steel. I've never witnessed a Viking berserker at work. But the last thing that enemy will ever see is his manic grin.

None of our foes even try to reach me. Makes me wonder if Marc told them he wanted to kill me himself.

Lucas raises his axe and joins the skirmish. The sharp edge of its blade almost tearing the nearest body in two. Such a messy way to kill someone. The blood coating the head of his axe turns to dust in an instant. He was supposed to wait for his brother to appear. To save himself for that fight. But the chance of him standing idly by was never good.

All I can hear is the bang of guns firing and the clang of steel meeting steel. It's a deafening cacophony. Ash from bodies sits in piles throughout the room. I keep my back to the wall and wait with my gun in hand to see if I can actually help. Though, the three of them are cutting through our enemies with relative ease. Give or take the odd wound from bullet or blade.

Such slaughter is overwhelming. No matter all of the death I've seen so recently. That it's happening here in our home is...there has to be a word stronger than disconcerting. Though, it does kind of sum it up. This was our safe place and now it's being invaded.

Marc at long last makes his appearance—and yes. This is what I want. For this asshole to have the final death. To be nothing more than an unpleasant old memory. Guess I *have* gotten bloodthirsty in a few different ways.

He's dressed in a three-piece suit. Very showy. The way he searches the room and then sneers at me doesn't improve the situation at all. Should Lucas fail to stop him, the creature is absolutely going to tear me to shreds. And I highly doubt my gun and I could stop one as ancient as him.

"She won't live to see another night," he says. "I promise it."

Lucas' shrug is nonchalant as fuck. But I am wise to his ways now. Hiding his heart is a given. It's what this world taught him is safe.

Marc snarls in anger.

The force with which Lucas charges him with his axe is breathtaking. And Marc meets him with a morning star. A type of club with a spiked metal ball attached to the top. Something I have only ever seen in a medieval movie about the crusades.

They're apparently in no rush, given how long the two have waited to kill each other. Because I can see their movements. Weapons being wielded like they're extensions of their bodies. Centuries of practice gives the fight a particular grace. Their skill may well be unrivaled by any other, undead or alive. Despite, or maybe due to their dexterity, neither successfully manages to land a blow. And after a minute or two, they step back from the bout, seemingly by unspoken consensuses, and each sets their weapon on the ground.

Marc growls in my general direction. Like he hasn't got enough going on in his life right now. Then he leaps at Lucas, and the two crash together again. I swear the ground shakes from their fury. Their hands hammer and claw at each other. Demons set loose from Hell couldn't seek more destruction. The brothers' hatred for one another is all-consuming. Bone cracks and blood flows, but neither stops or even pauses.

Henry and Benedict must have disposed of the rest of the thugs. Both are wounded, but the rest of our enemies are gone. They don't interfere in the ongoing fight between the brothers, however. No matter how much I might like them to help. My own complete lack of skill with a gun rules me out, too. Our maker is on his own. He probably wants it this way, but I do not have to like it.

Which is when an unhappy thought occurs to me. There's a small to medium chance I may have emotions happening when it comes to Lucas. Things beyond irritation and anger and outrage. Because the panic I experience as he faces such peril is extreme. On the verge of a total meltdown on my part. The thing is...I haven't heard all of his stories. I don't know as much about him as I would like. And the idea of our time together being brought to an abrupt end is fucking awful. I am this close to messy crying as the two brothers wage war against each other.

Having some sort of feelings for this monster isn't the worst thing in the world. The idea of us being important to each other. It doesn't need to mean anything big or unwieldy. This is fine.

Then, a full moment later, as Marc is pummeling his brother's face, I realize such a thought is absolute nonsense. Just complete rubbish. Because the truth is, I have somehow managed to stumble and fall in love with Lucas. So clumsy of me. But he has my whole, undead heart. I have never felt this way about anyone, living or dead, and I cannot lose him. He has to win. Anything else is untenable.

Just then, Lucas punches his hand through his brother's chest. Reaching up and under his rib cage to get at his heart. Marc's face contorts. He shrieks his rage and pain to the room. All of his people are dust, however. There's no one to come to his aid; no family or friends to help him. He is as alone in this moment as he can be. Lucas all but tears his brother in two. And the bloody body in his hands turns to ash as we watch.

Marc is dead. Deader. And thank fuck for that.

A muscle in the side of Lucas's jaw shifts, and his cool, clear blue gaze finds mine. Cuts and bruises spread across his skin diminish and change shades. The man has taken a beating. But he's still here. He's going to be okay.

We stare at each other for a long minute. There's a question in his eyes, and for once I don't turn away or make excuses. It doesn't matter that we've only known each other for a week. Or that there's an age gap between us as wide as the sea. He wants to be with me, and I want to be with him.

Seems there might be something to this soul mate's thing after all. I don't know how else to explain it. The slow smile spreading across his lips is everything. We survived. We really are going to be okay. It hardly even matters that our home is in ruins. Pottery pieces scattered on the ground. Paintings pockmarked with bullet holes. And don't even get me started on all of the beautiful books. Ugh.

I'm not even as upset anymore about him killing me. Because this new life I am living is kind of great. Give or take the occasional outbreaks of excessive violence, etcetera. He definitely requires further ongoing education regarding consent and equality, however.

"You're smiling," he says to me.

"Yeah. We're okay. We're still here."

"Of course."

Lucas might have taken our winning as a given. But I sure as hell had my concerns. I look around the room. "All of your stuff."

"I have more stuff," he says.

"So much more.. I'd like to see your brother come back from that," murmurs Henry, inspecting the pile of ash at their feet.

Lucas just grunts.

"Oh, no," says a still heavily bleeding Benedict in a sad voice. "Skye didn't get to shoot anyone."

Henry sighs. "That is a shame."

"She shouldn't have to miss out." Benedict is seriously aggrieved. "Why don't you shoot Henry now? I'll hold him down for you."

"Very funny," says Henry.

I just smile. "No. Thank you."

"I won't help you dig the bullets out of your stomach and leg if you're not nice to me, Benedict. I am warning you."

Lucas ignores them and wipes the dust off his hands as he crosses the room. He leans down and I reach up, and we meet in the middle. As it should be. No idea how bruised and battered his mouth might be. But I kiss him gently. And the kiss is a promise of so much more. Years and eons and all the rest. I really feel like this just might work out for us.

There's a light in his eyes as he says, "Skye can shoot someone next time we have another of these get-togethers."

Benedict just nods.

But I laugh. "Next time." Then, I stop laughing. "Wait. You're not serious, are you?"

# ☾ EPILOGUE

"What word am I thinking of?" asks Lucas, lounging on our bed.

I meet his gaze in the mirror as I finish brushing my hair. "The same word you're always thinking of."

"You need the practice, Skye. Come on."

"It's just going to be *sex*."

"It might not be."

"But it will be."

His lazy smile...the vampire is too handsome for his own good. "But it might not be."

Over a month has passed since the showdown with Marc. The house has mostly been set back to rights. Though, we still find shards of broken glass and stray cushion feathers here and there. Henry likes to call it war confetti.

Lucas has been to several board meetings, and the overhaul of The Boulevard Hotel is ongoing. Things seem to have calmed down in the city of angels. For the moment, at least.

"You haven't asked about the jewelry box sitting on your bedside table," he says, reaching for same.

Turns out he was right about owning more belongings. The vampire seems to have limitless resources. And he's been showering me with gifts. I feel like an undead Cinderella. In the space of a couple of months, I have gone from desperately needing to ask for a raise, to independently wealthy with a ridiculously rich boyfriend.

We've barely spent a moment apart since reaching our understanding and acknowledging our attachment. I don't know how Rose and Samuel handle a bond like this. How they managed to go for years living in separate countries. Guess it eases with time. Or perhaps you grow accustomed to the way it has its hooks so deep in your heart, there's no escaping it. But Lucas and I stay as close to each other as possible. I still don't know if soul mates are real. I just know I'm happier with him by my side.

The only upset during the last month came care of photos taken at my funeral. Helena sent the parcel. It was my decision whether to view the shots or not. Leave them for a decade, maybe, when the hurt wasn't so close to the surface.

My curiosity won out in the end. I hate how my family are grieving me. The sorrow on my mother's face will stay with me for the rest of time.

How my ex turned up and ugly cried at the service is wild. I mean, he dumped me. My best friend Nicole should have accidentally tripped and pushed him into my open grave. It's the least he deserves.

But Henry was right about the funeral being an end to that life. There's a certain comfort in knowing it is done, and my friends and family are hopefully moving on now. I don't know. Life and death are so complicated.

Apparently, as I'd hoped, my parents are buying a house on the beach with the life insurance payout. And I'm glad to hear it.

But back to the here and now.

Lucas tosses me the red velvet box from the side table. And I actually manage to catch it. "What's this?"

"Open it and see. Then tell me what word is on my mind."

I have been practicing reading minds and emotions. Strengthening the ability is going to take some time. But I no longer need to wait for the word to appear. I can now usually search it out on my own. Something which will, no doubt, come in use in this new life.

Inside the velvet box is an antique platinum and solitaire diamond ring. And it is awe inspiring. The sort of thing royalty wore in days of yore.

I don't know what to say. He's given me necklaces and bracelets and earrings. But this is the first time he's presented me with a ring. The thing is...it looks like an engagement ring. I highly doubt he intends for us to get hitched. Lucas has been single for well over a millennia. While we've been officially dating and living together for a whole month. A really great month. But still.

"I picked it up from Cartier in London near the start of the last century," he says, calm as can be.

"It's beautiful."

"Hmm. I am glad you like it. Read my mind, Skye."

And if the word he's thinking is either *sex* or *penis*, I am absolutely throwing the velvet box at him. Not the ring, though. It is far too pretty to be so abused.

I search for the quiet corner in my mind and then reach out to him. It's like there's a tentative bridge between his brain and mine. I don't know how else to describe the sensation.

His emotions find me first and shock the shit out of me. The man is actually nervous, despite the cool smile on his face and the at-ease body language. Being the Woodsman taught him to show a strong front at all times. To allow no vulnerabilities and to hide his fears. Never has he been nervous about a damn thing since I've known him. At least, I don't think he has. But he definitely is now.

Because the word he's giving me is *marriage*.

My carefully styled eyebrows reach for the roof. "What?"

He just watches me.

"Wow..."

And he still says nothing.

The sensible thing to do would be to wait for a year or two. To give ourselves time to ensure this is something lasting and real. But fuck that noise. "You know I love you, right?"

He cocks his head. "No. I didn't know. I suspected it. But I am happy to hear the words from your lips."

"You really want to get married?"

"I thought it might be something you would enjoy."

"Something I would enjoy?" I smile. "Lucas, you don't have to hide your heart from me."

"*You* are my heart, Skye. There is no hiding from you as much as I might like to."

Yeah. I don't know what to say. Because he has just delivered the most swoon-worthy line I have ever heard. Seriously.

Meanwhile, not knowing what to say is not a problem Henry is having out in the hallway. "Did she say yes?"

"Surely she would," Benedict's rumbly voice comes next. "Our sister is a very sensible woman, and the old man can support her in more than adequate comfort."

"Such a romantic way of looking at things. They love each other," says Leilah. "I'm sure it will be fine."

"How many of you, exactly, are listening at the door?" I ask, sliding the ring onto the appropriate finger.

"We've got Nico on the phone," reports Henry. "He wants an update. Yes or no, sweetie? You wouldn't believe the engagement party I have planned. Fireworks, champagne fountains, llamas, you name it."

"Llamas?"

The corner of Lucas's mouth has curled up some. And his gaze is glued to the ring on my hand. "Skye's answer is yes."

A hearty round of applause comes from the hallway. Having a happy family is a good thing.

Lucas is standing behind me in the blink of an eye. He wraps a hand around my ponytail and brushes his lips over my neck, making shivers race up my spine. His other arm wraps around my middle, anchoring my back to his front. One of the absolute best places in the world to be. I mesh my fingers with his and hold on tight. Tight enough that he couldn't get away if he tried.

"You don't have to read my mind," he whispers in my ear. "The next word is *forever*."

"*Forever*." I repeat with a smile. "I like that word."

Continue reading for a sneak peek of TEXT APPEAL

## Chapter One

If I hadn't been bored and lonely, I'd never have answered the text. But I sent out my new number hours ago and only three people responded. My mother, a guy I'd ghosted, and Grandpa. He sent a fire emoji. It's his answer to everything: Dad sharing his recipe for apple and walnut salad, Cousin Charlie and their partner getting engaged, Great Uncle Doug dying in his sleep... No one knows for sure what he thinks it means, but it enriches the family chat to no end.

But back to me and my sad state. My body might be worn out from hauling my belongings up three flights of stairs (boo to the broken elevator), however, my mind is wide awake. Though that's not unusual. Insomnia sucks.

Time to check my cell for the hundredth time. There were so many promises to keep in touch from my various friends and acquaintances, but they're not responding. They're probably out hitting the bars before heading to brunch in the morning, as per usual. Every weekend at home is the same. Heck. Every day is the same. Which is why, despite being allergic to change, I have made the move from a city in the desert to a small town on the coast.

All my life I've dreamed of living by the sea. Most of my childhood was spent watching *The Little Mermaid*, *SpongeBob SquarePants*, and *The Blue Planet*. And to think—it only took me twenty-nine years to get my shit together. While the fantasy was a lighthouse shrouded in mist sitting above a jagged coastline, an apartment on Main Street also works. The lease is for three months. More than enough time to figure out if I belong in the Pacific Northwest.

Like any self-respecting small town, things quiet down after nine when the restaurants close. Though some bars stay open, since it's Saturday. Two hours from the nearest city, there's no hum of traffic. But there are still many new noises to distract me and keep me from settling in. The salt wind racing past the big old brick building. The faint strains of jazz music coming from a neighbor's apartment. And the delightful chime of my cell receiving a text.

> **Unknown:** You can't just ignore me. We need to talk.
>
> **Me:** Wrong number.
>
> **Unknown:** C'mon, Connor.
>
> **Me:** No one named Connor here. You have the wrong number.
>
> **Unknown:** Stop lying to me. We've known each other too long for this shit.
>
> **Me:** But not long enough for him to give you his new number, apparently.
>
> **Unknown:** Ouch. No. I don't believe it. There's no way you'd give up boobs.
>
> **Me:** Boobs?

**Unknown:** The last five digits of the number. 80085

**Me:** Ha. I hadn't noticed.

**Unknown:** He's had it since high school. It was his juvenile pride and joy.

**Me:** Maybe he finally outgrew it.

**Unknown:** Hang on. You're his new girlfriend, aren't you?

**Me:** No again.

**Unknown:** I don't believe you.

**Me:** Okay.

**Unknown:** You admit it?

**Me:** Nope. Just acknowledging that being wrong is a choice you can make. It's your life.

**Unknown:** Giving you his cell and getting you to deal with me sounds about right. The last time we spoke he was not happy. Do you make him happy?

**Me:** I don't even know him.

**Unknown:** I don't believe you. Things have changed. Tell him I need to talk to him.

**Me:** He still isn't here.

**Unknown:** I wouldn't give him the cell either if I was you.

**Me:** When did you two last actually talk?

**Unknown:** Christmas.

**Me:** Yikes. That's months. The relationship sounds broken. Have you thought about putting it in a bag of rice?

**Unknown:** Very funny. Time for another drink. Hotel mini bars are the best. I don't usually get to meet his female friends. Guess I should introduce myself.

**Unknown:** Hi. I'm Ava. What's your name?

*Hmm.* Logic would suggest I block her and move on with my life. As sad, pathetic, and sleepless as it might currently be. However, writers are notoriously nosy creatures. Especially when it comes to relationship drama, and I write romance.

**Me:** Riley.

**Ava:** Nice to meet you. Sort of.

**Me:** I don't know your story, but is he worth all the angst?

**Ava:** You haven't heard about me? Are you new to Port Stewart?

**Me:** You're from Port Stewart?

**Ava:** Yeah. Born and bred. Connor and I were high school sweethearts and we've been on and off ever since.

**Me:** How long is that now?

**Ava:** Fifteen years. Are you planning on staying in town?

I hesitate again. It's one thing to exchange nonsense texts with a random stranger. However, giving details about my life and location doesn't feel safe. Not that she has asked me anything which might identify my new address. The conversation just seems weird suddenly. Weirder. You would think area codes cover a decent distance. What are the odds these people would be local?

**Me:** As my mother says, drink a glass of water before you go to bed.

**Ava:** You seem nice. But he will come back to me. He always does.

**Me:** Okay. Good night, Ava.

**Ava:** See you soon, Riley.

And that doesn't sound ominous at all.

My previous phone number was spammed out of existence. Just endless nuisance calls and texts trying to scam me. It had to go. I wonder why Connor changed his—if it had anything to do with his ex. Or maybe he decided to throw his cell into the sea. To shun the modern world and do away with technology. It's not a bad idea. Though the Ava situation seems more likely. The timing is certainly curious, what with her coming back to town. Imagine having over a decade's worth of romantic conflict with someone. It really takes it beyond second-chance romance and into the realm of complicated as fuck. But why wouldn't he just block her?

I've dated a variety of people over the years. None of them lasted long. And the only on-again, off-again relationship I have is with tequila—we're toxic together.

Thanks to the texting, I am now more awake than ever. Time to take another stroll through my new place. The apartment came furnished. There's a solid-wood dining set, a chunky gray sofa, and an old-style black metal bed frame. As for the rest, it's basically a blank canvas. The walls are white, the floors are polished wood, and the kitchen counters are dark stone. Mom would immediately cover the place with bright throws and pillows. But I am going to sit with the space for a few days and see how it feels.

There's not much of a view from the bedroom, but the large windows in the living/dining/kitchen space more than make up for it. A full moon is shining down on the bay. There's something mystical about the way the water moves in the moonlight. How dark shadows show the ebb and flow. I still can't believe I am here. Going from a city in the desert to a small coastal town is going to be an experience. Having whole-ass states between me and the place I used to call home. But I wanted to challenge myself. To be somewhere totally new.

"You can do this," I tell my reflection in the window. "It is going to be great."

It rained all day Sunday, making it perfect weather for settling in and unpacking. My first official outing takes place on Monday morning. I've tied back my shoulder-length light blue hair (necessitated by precipitation making it bouffant and fluffy as fuck), and am wearing jeans and a white tee. The goal is to look like a local—to blend and belong. Though while people-watching through my window I observed an array of styles. From hiking gear to ren faire to quiet luxury and back again. The population might only be five thousand, but they clearly come from all walks of life.

Out on the street, the sky is clear, and a cool breeze blows off the water. The scent of salt and sea fills the air, and I hear gulls crying. My heart feels two sizes too big, straining at the bars of my rib cage, and my smile can barely fit on my face. Being here, making my dream come true, is amazing.

My new apartment is in an old, ornate building with stores on the ground floor. A secondhand bookseller and an ice cream parlor. It's how I knew this was the place. Books and sugar—an unbeatable combination.

There hasn't been a single communication for Connor this morning. No texts or calls or nothing. Guess he's sent out a new number, since I doubt everyone suddenly stopped talking to the man. His plethora of messages from yesterday include:

Any news on the mustang?

Grab some beer if you're coming over to watch the game.

You were right. The bronco is dead as a doornail.

Any idea on the numbers for the party? Will the back room be big enough or should we have it in the bar?

Are we still on for Seattle tomorrow?

Let me know when you and Ava can come to dinner.

This was followed by a selfie from the woman herself, along with a message wishing Connor and me a great weekend. Which is funny in a shit-stirring sort of way. Her long dark hair shines and her olive skin is flawless, and I don't even think it's a filter. Ava really is the worst.

Next was a voice message from his mother asking when he's picking up Ava from the airport and if she should make her blackberry cobbler or hazelnut bread for the welcome home party. Apparently his mother is unaware of their relationship status.

And last but not least, my personal favorite, a late-night booty call. Which is how I met my new friend, Yumi. She's an accountant in a neighboring town and knew all the great places to eat and visit. I asked her about Connor, but all she would say is that she doesn't call him for conversation.

I should have just turned off my phone. It would have been the sensible thing to do. But receiving random details about this man's life is fascinating. The mustang and bronco mentions are particularly interesting—makes me wonder if Connor is a cowboy. You have to appreciate someone who knows their way around a length of rope and is good with their hands. Of course, he might just be a general horse enthusiast. Either would be fine with me.

So far, I've received a thumbs up on the change of number from a school friend who moved to Missouri, and a slightly harsh *Who is this?* from an old college roommate. Such is life. Some fellow authors messaged to check that I had arrived in one piece. Which is nice.

The relative quiet over my new number announcement has made me think that maybe I'm to blame for the lack of meaningful connections in my life. I've been focused on building my business for the past five years.

As I walk down the block, I smile at the people I pass. And some even smile back. My goals for the day are thus: coffee, check out the local area, grocery shop, and get my word count done. Find new friends, true love, and the meaning of life would also be great. However, I'll settle for managing to make conversation with at least one person in real life. I could use the practice.

The espresso machine hissing and spitting behind the counter in the Main Street Coffee House is a beautiful thing. And a number of people are gathered waiting, which is a good sign. Colorful paintings share wall space with notices for local events and some of the windows are stained glass. There's also a whole lot of beautiful, lush potted plants. I am officially obsessed.

Soup and salad are listed on the chalkboard menu, and sandwiches and pastries fill a glass cabinet. Music plays and people chat. The overall vibe is so warm and welcoming. I can see myself working at one of the small wooden tables tucked away in a corner and gorging on coffee and cake.

"What can I get you?" asks the smiling barista when I finally reach the front of the line.

"A cold brew and a chocolate chip cookie, thanks."

"Sure thing."

She's older than me and the embroidery on her tee says Shanti. Her skin is umber, and her hair is in Dutch braids. I pass her a twenty-dollar bill and she hands back the change. Now is the time to make friends by tipping big, and they're doing dueling jars. How cool. The pizza place back home did this all the time. Things like boxers versus briefs or cats versus dogs.

Here, however, one tip jar reads *AVA THE HOMETOWN HERO* and the other says *RILEY THE NEW GIRL*.

*What the fuck?*

"Your name?" asks the waitress with a pen and a cardboard coffee cup in hand.

It cannot be real. I blink repeatedly, but the scene before me doesn't change. What are the chances there's another Riley in town who was recently accused of dating a certain dude? Ava has obviously been talking and texting up a storm.

When she sees me staring at the jars, Shanti sighs. "That's just some local nonsense. Don't pay it any mind."

"There's only a nickel in the new girl's jar, but the other one is almost full."

Shanti rests her hip against the counter while giving the other barista serious side eye. "Some people are mistaking real life for one of those damn reality dating shows."

"It's funny," says the second barista, a young white man.

"Are you still going to think it's funny when Connor finds out?" asks an older man in waders standing at the end of the counter.

The smile falls off the young man's face. "That dude doesn't have a sense of humor."

"Not lately, he doesn't. But he said he'd help you with the colt so you might want to try a little harder to stay on his good side." Shanti turns back to me and says, "Your order won't be long."

I shove the few bills I have in my purse, along with some coins I find rolling around, into the new girl jar. It's everything I have on me. Then I hide off to the side behind a particularly verdant fern. Shock is the prevailing emotion. I've only been in town for two days. How the hell have I already become part of the local discourse?

This could well sink my plans for debuting a new-and-improved seaside version of me. One who knows how to socialize, amongst other things. While I don't have an exact outline for Riley 2.0, I would also appreciate it if I could stop randomly saying the wrong thing and regularly spilling crap on myself. Of course, it's the dream to be cool, calm, and confident. Though I am pretty sure hiding behind foliage in public rules out those three. And what has never been on my list is becoming a man-thieving ho.

"I think it's fate," says the grizzled old man in fishing gear. "The way Ava and Connor keep finding their way back to each other."

A silver-haired woman holding a designer handbag and wearing three strands of pearls around her neck nods thoughtfully.

"That's very romantic of you, Harold." Shanti plates up a pastry. "I didn't know you had it in you."

But the next person in line groans loudly. "Please. She's always leaving. I don't know why he keeps taking her back."

"She's a successful modern woman," answers Harold with his head held high. "It's not her fault her work takes her places."

Another person in athleisure adds a quarter to the jar. "My money goes to new girl."

It's not much, but I'll take it. With silent thanks.

"You're both just still pissed Ava got prom queen." A man with a toddler on his hip stuffs a dollar bill into the other jar. Dammit.

"Way to swear in front of the baby, Wade," says Shanti.

"She was also captain of the girls' baseball team, lead in the school musical, and Miss Port Stewart." Harold counts off each accomplishment on his fingers. "This new girl, whoever she is, would have to be pretty special to compare."

And the bitch of it is, the bulk of them agree.

But my hero, athleisure woman, shakes her head vehemently. "All of those things happened over fifteen years ago."

"It's not as if she's been slacking since," says Harold.

No one argues the point. Shit. Small wonder the contents of my jar are so meager. I'm up against an overachieving beauty queen. I came second in a talent show once. My performance of "The Cup Song" was solid. But that was my peak, school achievements-wise. That and being accused of plagiarism by a teacher because the story I wrote for class was too good.

This is all unsettling. Maybe I should tell them the truth. How Ava texted me and jumped to the wrong conclusion. Though it would be my word against the hometown heroine. What's the likelihood I would be believed?

Two tourists enter the coffee shop. One holds a camera while the other studies a brochure. There are lots of hotels and inns along the waterfront. Port Stewart is a popular place. There're plenty of restaurants, art and culture, history, and scenery to recommend it. And it's only two hours from Seattle.

"We're looking for the farmers market?" asks the man.

"The corner of Hemlock and Lawrence," answers Shanti. "But it's only on Saturdays."

The now sad-faced tourists shuffle back out.

Shanti picks up a cookie with a napkin and places it into a paper bag. "Where is...there you are. Your order's ready. I never did get your name."

I rush over and reach for my coffee and cookie. Only sugar and caffeine can save this day. "Thank you very much."

"You're very welcome."

It's not far to the door. Fifteen feet or so at most. Good thing I wore flats. While I don't exactly run, I don't exactly walk either. My cold brew sloshes about inside the paper cup.

Time for a new plan. I shall weather the storm by valiantly hiding out in my apartment until this shit blows over. It's not like I have any problems hunkering down and introverting. Ava will return and be reunited with Connor and talk will turn to something else. Something that doesn't involve me. Then I will forget about this shit, relaunch my seaside life, and all will be splendid.

Before I can reach it, however, the coffee shop door swings open and in walks the building superintendent. The same person who gave me the keys to my new apartment. Her face lights up at the sight of me and she loudly proclaims, "Hey there, Riley!"

Purchase from your favorite online retailer today!

# PURCHASE KYLIE SCOTT'S OTHER BOOKS

*Text Appeal*

*The Last Days of Lilah Goodluck*

*End of Story*
*Beginning of the End* (Prequel Novella)

*Famous in a Small Town*

## THE WEST HOLLYWOOD SERIES
*Fake*

*Love Under Quarantine*

*The Rich Boy*

*Lies*

## THE LARSEN BROTHERS SERIES
*Repeat*
*Pause*

*It Seemed Like a Good Idea at the Time*

*Trust*

**THE DIVE BAR SERIES**
*Dirty*
*Twist*
*Chaser*

**THE STAGE DIVE SERIES**
*Lick*
*Play*
*Lead*
*Deep*
*Strong: A Stage Dive Novella*

**THE FLESH SERIES**
*Flesh*
*Skin*
*Flesh Series Novellas*

*Heart's a Mess*

*Colonist's Wife*

# ABOUT KYLIE SCOTT

Kylie is a *New York Times*, *Wall Street Journal*, and *USA Today* best-selling, Audie Award winning author. She has sold over 2,000,000 books and was voted Australian Romance Writer of the year four times by the Australian Romance Reader's Association. Her books have been translated into sixteen different languages. She is based in Queensland, Australia; living and working on land traditionally owned by the Jagera people.

www.kyliescott.com
Facebook: www.facebook.com/kyliescottwriter
Instagram: www.instagram.com/kylie_scott_books
Pinterest: www.pinterest.com/kyliescottbooks
BookBub: www.bookbub.com/authors/kylie-scott

\*\*To learn about exclusive content,
upcoming releases and giveaways,
join Kylie Scott's newsletter:
https://kyliescott.com/subscribe\*\*